'**How lo**

Unable to understand why Tony had asked, Sarah stared at him, and saw the silver eyes darken to a steely grey. She forced herself to breathe evenly, definitely not pant, for his eyes has darkened in just that way when they'd made love.

'A month. I've three more weeks,' she told him.

The smile this time was totally different— slow and seductive—but its effect was like a blowtorch as it scorched across her skin and sent more heat into her blood.

'And I've three days,' he said softly.

He reached out, drew her close, and kissed her firmly on the lips.

'Tomorrow,' he said, making the word a promise.

As a person who lists her hobbies as 'reading, reading and reading', it was hardly surprising **Meredith Webber** fell into writing when she needed a job she could do at home. Not that anyone in the family considers it a 'real' job! She is fortunate enough to live on the Gold Coast in Queensland, Australia, as this gives her the opportunity to catch up with many other people with the same 'unreal' job when they visit the popular tourist area.

Recent titles by the same author:

LOVE ME*
TRUST ME*
AN ENTICING PROPOSAL
A HUGS-AND-KISSES FAMILY**

Trilogy
**Bundles of Joy*

MARRY ME

BY

MEREDITH WEBBER

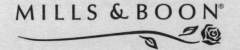

First published in Great Britain 2000
Harlequin Mills & Boon Limited,
Eton House, 18-24 Paradise Road, Richmond, Surrey TW9 1SR

© Meredith Webber 2000

ISBN 0 263 82250 8

Set in Times Roman 10½ on 11¼ pt.
03-0007-53540

Printed and bound in Spain
by Litografia Rosés, S.A., Barcelona

CHAPTER ONE

'ARE you going to the McMurrays' cocktail party tonight?'

Sarah Gilmour turned from the wash-basin and considered her friend rather than the question. Emmie North had been a nursing sister at Windrush Sidings' small hospital twelve years ago when Sarah, with Lucy in tow, had arrived to take up the job of resident doctor.

Lucy had been seven, an excitable sprite, unaware of her mother's fears and concerns about how a small community would accept a doctor who was not only a woman but also an unmarried mother.

It had been Sarah's first country appointment, the first time she'd had sole responsibility for a hospital. Emmie, three years older and about a hundred years wiser, had been her guide and mentor.

Now Sarah was back to do a four-week locum, and Emmie was still here, still guiding and mentoring.

Still trying to organise Sarah's private life!

'Well?' Emmie prompted.

'I don't know, Em,' Sarah said. 'It's been a hectic week. I need a quiet night with my feet up in front of the telly more than I need the social hoo-ha of a McMurray cocktail party.'

More than I need the strain of facing Stewart McMurray.

'But it's the opening bash of the weekend. Everyone will be there,' Emmie protested.

Everyone but me, Sarah thought, but she didn't say it because she knew Emmie would keep pressing if she said a definite no.

'Lucy might be here in time for it,' Emmie suggested. 'If she is, she'll want to go.'

Sarah smiled as she thought of her daughter. 'Only if James is also in town,' she reminded her friend.

'Oh, so that's still on?'

'Still on?' Sarah sighed. 'I doubt it's ever been really *on*, Emmie, in the sense you mean. Lucy has always adored him, although she assures me it's friendship, nothing else. A friendship that began right here, and developed into something special.'

'He was so kind to her when she was little,' Emmie remarked. 'I guess he was a lonely kid, growing up out there on his own, no brothers or sisters. Do you remember when she first started school here and had a fight with some boy who took her apple? I'll never forget James walking her back to the hospital. Her school uniform was torn, one plait was undone, and she had more dirt on her face than on the soles of her shoes. Yet he treated her as if she were a princess.'

'*And* told me, quite seriously, that I should be very proud of her because she'd won the fight,' Sarah added. 'You know, I'd forgotten all about that!'

'That's because you've tried to blank Windrush Sidings out of your mind. Bad business, shutting things away. You lose a heap of happy memories as well.'

Sarah smiled at the woman who'd become one of her closest friends, the relationship maintained through phone calls, letters and Emmie's holiday visits to the coast where Sarah and Lucy had their home.

'OK! No nagging. I'm back here now and quite prepared to review at least some of those happy memories. Although returning this particular week has been a baptism of fire. The town's gone crazy with the one-hundred-and-fifty-year anniversary. I've had to do more patching and sewing than they would at the quilt club.'

'It's because nothing much ever happens out here—except for the doom-laden stuff like floods and fires and drought. We've had more than our fair share of natural disasters over the years, but this time the town's excited because it's attracting attention for a good reason, not a bad one. A hundred and fifty years' survival in harsh bush country like ours is worth celebrating.'

Emmie's love for her home town, and her enthusiasm for the upcoming event, sparkled in her eyes.

'So don't be a spoilsport. Come to the party. Apart from anything else, it will give you a chance to see Alana queening it as the town's leading lady. It might have taken a few years to get the wedding ring on her finger, but I bet she was in Stewart's bed before poor Anna was cold in her grave.'

She stopped as suddenly as if someone had thrown a switch to turn her off then muttered, 'Gosh, I'm sorry. Tactless of me, bringing Anna into the conversation.'

'Someone had to, some time,' Sarah told her. 'It's been a long time, Emmie, and I'm all grown up now. I can handle things a darn sight better now than I did then.'

She turned back to the sink and finished washing her hands, hoping her assertion was correct and that she would be able to handle the social side of life in Windrush Sidings.

'I'll check Toddy and if he's feeling OK send him home,' Emmie said, turning their conversation to work-related matters.

'No, you finish up and go get ready for the party. I'll see him and do a quick visit to the ward. Bessie Sinclair's looking very frail.'

'It's sheer tenacity that's keeping her alive for the festivities,' Emmie replied. 'If she dies, her sister Nell will be interviewed as the Sidings' oldest resident and she's only one hundred to Bessie's one hundred and two. The pair of them have always fought, so Bessie'd be mortified to give Nell the opportunity!'

She walked towards the door of the scrub room, then turned back to Sarah.

'I *will* see you at the McMurrays'?'

Sarah shrugged, then, knowing Emmie would persist, said, 'Most probably. Providing no one else electrocutes himself, putting up party lights, or amputates a digit, cutting eucalypt branches for the decorations outside his shop, or burns herself on the barbecues set up for ''Breakfast in the Park'' tomorrow morning.'

Emmie grinned at her.

'It *has* been a hectic first week for you, hasn't it? Never mind, in a few days it will all be over, and Windrush will go back to sleep for another fifty years. Think you'll make the two-hundred-year celebrations?'

'I think Bessie and Nell have more chance of that than me, the way I feel at the moment,' Sarah told her.

Emmie departed, leaving Sarah to reflect on her own remark. Although she *was* tired, it wasn't so much the busy week that had affected her equilibrium. A jittery feeling had developed as she'd driven into town to face her ghosts. It had grown to a fully fledged uneasiness, walking beside her through each day and disrupting her sleep with unwanted dreams each night.

'It's good to have you here again,' Toddy said, when she went to check on the publican who'd grabbed a live wire while stringing party lights outside the hotel in readiness for the big weekend.

'Good to have *you* here,' Sarah teased him. He'd been lucky because his wife, knowing his foolhardiness with electricity, had stationed herself by the switch and had thrown it the moment the shock had hit him. Apart from three burnt fingers, now neatly wrapped in dry dressings, he was as good as new. 'No more heroics, please.'

'No time for any more fussing,' he assured her. 'The party starts tonight.'

'You're going out to the McMurrays'? I thought you'd be too busy at the pub.'

Toddy winked at her.

'That's where the real party will be,' he said. 'At the pub. You'll be most welcome to come along, Doc, and you'll meet more real people than you will out at Craigmoor. Not that Stewart hasn't always been approachable in a lordly kind of way, but that Alana! Talk about airs and graces. You'd think her—' He stopped abruptly, but not before Sarah's mind had finished the colloquialism for him. She smiled, not at the expression but at Toddy not saying it in front of her.

'I'll think about the pub party,' she promised, 'although after what amounted to an all-nighter last night with Shelley Smith's baby, I'm really too tired to be going anywhere.'

'You'll have to eat,' Toddy reminded her. 'Dinner on the house.' He stood up and put out his hand. 'See you later, then,' he said, shaking hands with great formality. 'And thanks, Doc.'

Sarah watched him go, and realised his attitude was what she liked about small country hospitals. The doctor was accepted by everyone in town. Not revered or treated as someone special, but welcomed as a friend—perhaps because the small hospitals were so hard to staff, and the locals, whose isolation made medical care important to them, were appreciative of anyone willing to serve their community.

She left the casualty room and walked through to the big airy ward, divided into men's and women's sections by a wide passage and the nurses' station.

'I'll make it through to Monday,' Bessie Sinclair assured her when she stopped by the old lady's bed.

'I'm sure you will,' Sarah agreed, but her patient's pulse was weak and thready. Had the anticipation of this big event taken the woman's last reserves of strength?

'Come and see me in the morning. Tell me about to-night's party,' Bessie said in a surprisingly strong voice. 'I'm only going to the street parade. On the hospital float, but not in bed like this. They've made a big throne for me. I'll sit on that.'

'It will be wonderful,' Sarah said. The street parade was to be the culmination of the weekend's festivities, the final event on the Monday public holiday. Sarah had learned about the construction of the float earlier in the week when it had left the wards empty of staff and she'd found herself answering calls for bedpans. For some reason the organisers had decided on a water theme, and an old car had been converted into a huge black swan with Bessie's 'throne' set into its chest below a curling neck and bright red beak.

In front of the throne was a shaky-looking deck, painted blue, where all the staff off duty during the vital hours intended to stand and wave. Sarah had excused herself from this gaiety, saying it was better she was available on the ground.

Now she spoke to the nurse on duty, asking to be called if Bessie showed signs of breathing difficulties or any sudden deterioration. Then, after a quick visit to Shelley and her baby in the two-bed 'maternity ward', Sarah crossed the yard behind the hospital, making her way to the little cottage, tucked away behind a screen of trees, that was her temporary home.

She considered her two invitations for the evening—a cocktail party or dinner at the pub—on the way.

As she pushed through the door, she realised she'd have to go to both or not go out at all. It was the only way she wouldn't offend either host.

'Surprise! Gosh, we thought you were never coming! We've been tucked away in here for ages.'

Lucy, just nineteen and brimming with youthful health and vitality, leapt from behind the kitchen divider and flung herself into Sarah's arms, hugging her tight. Sarah returned the embrace, welcoming the feel of her daughter's slight body, the scent of her hair, the aliveness of her.

'We?' she queried, then glanced over Lucy's shoulder and caught sight of James standing sheepishly by the sink.

'The surprise thing was her idea,' he said quickly, and Sarah grinned at him. She'd decided she liked James McMurray when he was nine, and her affection for him had deepened over the years.

'I'd have just as soon walked into the hospital to say hello in a less dramatic manner,' he added.

'And you a dramatist!' Lucy teased, but there was a new softness—a tenderness—in her voice.

Sarah felt her heart shift in her chest.

Was this what the jittery feeling had been about?

Had Lucy's friendship with James taken on a new dimension?

'He's just been announced as a finalist in the Young Playwright of the Year Awards and that play you read, the second one, has been bought by a real theatre company in Sydney,' Lucy announced.

'A real theatre company! I *am* impressed,' Sarah teased, putting out her arms to welcome him and enfolding the young man in a warm hug. 'So! I wasn't sure if you intended coming for the celebrations,' she said to him, although she now realised it was probably James's presence in town, not hers, that had brought Lucy on this visit.

'I wasn't going to come, but suddenly things are happening for me, Sarah, good things, and I decided I should at least try to heal the breach with Dad.'

Sarah smiled warmly at him.

'That's maturity speaking, James,' she said, as proud of him as she would have been of Lucy in the same situation. 'I'm glad.'

'Don't be too glad,' James warned. 'I'm not overly optimistic myself and I'm only one side of the equation. I doubt it will ever be truly healed because I have no intention of taking over Craigmoor, and Dad will never accept that a McMurray could shirk his duty and not live out his destiny as protector of the hallowed acres.'

'Well, at least you're trying to make things right between you,' she said softly, and she hugged him again, before turning back to her daughter. 'So, how's the study going? What's the news? Have you been down home lately?'

Lucy glanced at James before answering.

'We went down last weekend, but only for the day. Had a swim, checked the place wasn't falling down, lunched with the Grandies, then drove back to Armidale. They sent their love—the Grandies.'

The significance of the 'we' wasn't lost on Sarah, but she set it aside and asked about her parents—the Grandies to Lucy—about the house itself and the garden. She'd bought the little cottage by the ocean at Coffs Harbour when Lucy had decided she wanted to go to boarding school. Lucy's decision had been based on the fact that James, with whom she'd corresponded once they'd left Windrush Sidings, had been shunted off to an all-boys establishment that had a sister school in the same town.

Sarah had tried to talk her out of it, though eventually she'd realised the school might give Lucy more stability than she could have with her erratic hospital working hours. So holiday times had been special. Sarah had started working locums to ensure she'd had the school holidays free to spend with her daughter. And, more often than not, with James as well.

He'd begun to accompany Lucy to the beach house during the shorter holidays because it had been too far to travel to his home, then, gradually, he'd become a regular visitor over the long summer break as well, spending Christmas at Craigmoor before escaping to the beach as soon as possible after the celebrations.

'So, James, you'd better be off to beard the dragons in their den. And check it's OK with them for me to stay the night.' Lucy's command interrupted Sarah's thoughts.

'Mum, you're going to the party at Craigmoor, aren't you? We can have some time together while you get ready, then I'll drive out with you.'

Sarah smiled. Lucy had been born with an over-developed organisation gene, and had begun arranging Sarah's life almost as soon as she could talk.

'I hadn't decided whether I'd go or not,' Sarah protested.

'You'll go,' James told her. 'It's easier to fall in line than argue with your daughter. I learned that years ago.'

There was a fondness in his voice, but was there any more than that? Sarah felt a quiver of fear, and said a silent mother-prayer that her daughter would be spared heartache.

Not that prayers would help. Heartache was part of growing up, part of the rites of passage to womanhood.

'OK,' she agreed. 'But I won't stay long. If I go out there, I'll have to poke my head in at the pub as well or I'll be labelled a snob.'

'Well, I can tell you which party I'd rather be at,' James said gloomily, but Lucy's enthusiasm refused to be dampened.

'Nonsense!' she said, pushing him towards the door. 'There's one good thing to be said for Alana—and that's that she can cook! The food at your place will be super.'

James pecked Sarah's cheek and said, 'See you later.' Then he walked away with the slow, heavy tread of a man going to his doom.

'Have you pushed him into this reconciliation?' Sarah asked Lucy as he drove away.

'Who, me?' Lucy was all wide-eyed astonishment. 'Mum! How could you think such a thing?'

'Because I know you,' Sarah countered, then regretted her firmness when Lucy's face lost its bright beauty.

'Do you think it was wrong to encourage him to see his family? Should I have stayed out of it? Honestly, Mum, I would have, only I hadn't seen him for so long—he's been in Sydney with the company that's bought his play—and then he comes back to Armidale and finds a gift, an invitation to the celebrations, *and* a note from his father, asking him to please try to come. It's the first personal communication he's had since his twenty-first last February.'

Sarah thought about families divided, and her recent experiences in another small country town, and hastened to reassure her daughter.

'You did the right thing, encouraging him to come,' she said, then smiled as the brilliance returned to Lucy's eyes.

'Good,' Miss Organisation replied. 'Now, get dressed or we'll never get there.'

Get dressed?

What did one wear to cocktails when your last visit had been to pronounce the host's first wife dead?

Not that she had much choice. She had one all-purpose black shift dress, made of some man-made fibre which resisted crushing, stains and other destructive forces, including, she suspected, an atomic blast. With a string of pearls slung around her neck, it would be dressy enough for cocktails at the McMurrays', and if she took off the pearls it would pass for casual in the pub.

Aware that Lucy had the advantage of youth and could throw on any garment and look stunning within seconds, Sarah showered hurriedly so she could snatch an extra few minutes to put on make-up and do something with her hair.

'Come on, Mum, we're already late!'

Lucy slouched on the bed, her reed-slim body partly clad in a slinky little scrap of lilac organza over an even scrappier sheath of lush violet satin. Her hair, almost white blonde, was tucked behind her ear on one side and fell in a shining swathe across her eye on the other. Dark mascara and bright red lipstick were her only facial adornment, but she looked sensational.

And probably knew it!

Sarah felt her own hair sliding traitorously out of the

knot she was trying to fix to the top of her head, and sighed in exasperation.

'Blow it, it can stay down,' she muttered, and, seizing her hairbrush, she swiped it vigorously through the un-cooperative strands until the red-gold gleamed like shot silk against her pale skin and the dull black of her dress.

'You look about sixteen,' Lucy told her.

'Twenty-six would be nice. Have you packed your over-night things? Are you ready?'

'Ready? When I've been waiting hours for you?'

Lucy shrugged a small backpack over one shoulder and slid her free arm around her mother's waist, steering her towards the front door.

Sarah felt a rush of love so strong it made her knees go wobbly.

'It's so good to have you here, Luce,' she said huskily, then, as the arm around her waist tightened in reply, she added, 'Even if your reasons for coming weren't entirely due to daughterly love!'

Lucy opened the car door for her, then turned hesitantly towards her mother.

'Things have changed between James and me lately, Mum, but we're not lovers, you know.'

Do I?

And is that regret I hear in your voice?

Sarah slid into the driver's seat.

'You're OK about these changes?' she asked, looking anxiously up at her only chick.

'I'm orchestrating them, Mum,' the chick said, so youth-fully confident that Sarah felt a spasm of fear this time. But before she could find words of warning mild enough to be acceptable to Lucy, her daughter spoke again.

'You know I've no pride whatsoever where James is con-cerned,' she said, then added ruefully, 'I may or may not end up as his lover, but I will always be his friend, and he needs a friend tonight.' She paused for a moment, then added, 'The rest of it is my problem, Mum. *My* heartache, if things don't turn out the way I'd like. Don't worry about me.'

'Tell that to the wind!' Sarah told her when Lucy joined her in the car, and they headed out of town, driving west into the fiery extravagance of the sunset as the brilliant orange orb slipped towards the far-away horizon. 'Worrying about you isn't something I can switch on and off at will. All I can do is suffer in silence—well, almost in silence!'

She pulled a face to lighten the words—pretending she was teasing—and wondered about other pretences between parents and their offspring.

'I'll be OK!' Lucy assured her.

Sarah wished she had half her daughter's assurance as butterflies danced jigs in her stomach when they pulled through the gate to Craigmoor. While parking on the sweeping gravelled drive brought back so many memories that her knees started to behave badly again.

'OK, let's go tug our forelocks to the local gentry,' Lucy said. Her eagerness betrayed how anxious she was to be with James again, but as she'd been too young to remember the drama of James's mother's death and had holidayed at Craigmoor over the years, the place was free of ghosts—for her.

Sarah bent forward and pulled on the strappy sandals she's slipped off to make driving easier, then, lacking any further excuse for delay, she climbed out of the car and reluctantly accompanied her daughter towards the front entrance to the low-set stone and timber house.

Music reached out to welcome them and voices flowed through the wide glass doors that led out onto a pergola-shaded verandah.

Her stomach knotted with nerves, Sarah followed her eager daughter, up two steps and into the fray. A few guests had taken advantage of the balmy night and were outside, but the main gathering was in the long, wide room that ran across the front of the house, different clusters of furniture designating dining and sitting areas.

The polished cypress floorboards gleamed gold in the artificial light, and huge arrangements of flowers from Alana's garden gave the room a festive air. Across the heads of the guests Sarah saw the tall figure of their host, Stewart McMurray. He nodded a greeting but Sarah guessed from the suits surrounding him that he wouldn't be crossing the room to welcome them.

Then Lucy let out a glad cry of, 'Uncle Tony!' She darted from Sarah's side. Heading straight towards Stewart and the suits.

One suit in particular.

Sarah's knees, already suffering the after-effects of too much emotion in one day, all but buckled as a dark head turned towards Lucy, then beyond Lucy towards the door.

She caught a glint of silver in the black sheen of his hair as the head dipped in wry acknowledgement of her presence, just seconds before her daughter threw herself into the arms of the one man Sarah had never expected to see again.

Well, to be truthful, she'd kind of hoped. Indulged in dreams where one day they might meet as friends. She'd missed him, longed for him, and recently, when events had reminded her of what they'd had—and lost—even considered contacting him.

But to see him again like this, so unexpectedly…

And at Craigmoor, where their love had imploded with such force she'd sometimes wondered if she'd ever recover.

It was too much.

'Need a drink?'

She turned to find James beside her, and saw an understanding smile in his golden-brown eyes.

'If this was Lucy's doing…' Sarah began, and was glad when James shook his head.

'Not this time,' he assured her, 'but no doubt she's wondering why she didn't think of it. We haven't seen him for a couple of years—not since he was transferred to the city—although Lucy writes him reams.'

He eased his way through the crowd, leading Sarah towards a bar set up at the far end of the long room.

'Apparently, he's recently been appointed as the liaison between the police department and the State police minister—who happens to be Ned Burrows, Windrush's local parliamentarian. Ned's here as official Pooh-Bah for the celebrations and brought along an entourage. According to Tony, he's just making up the numbers for his boss. Actually, if it's any consolation, I think Dad was as put out over it as you are.'

Sarah was grateful for James's explanation as it gave her time to collect herself. Then, as he deposited her safely by the bar, and handed her, without asking her choice, a glass of chilled Riesling, she caught an anxious glint in his eyes.

'I'm OK,' she assured him, then grimaced. 'Well, almost OK. If ever you write a play about middle-aged women, bear in mind they can have equally as forceful a physical reaction to an appealing man as teenagers can.'

'Really?'

She grinned. That was the wonderful thing about James. He was always interested, no matter how banal or bizarre the conversation might be. It was if he stored the words and phrases in his head, ready to be used as building blocks in his plays.

'Really,' she affirmed. 'My knees went weak, my stomach turned over, my heart galloped unevenly about in my chest, and my breath most definitely got trapped in my lungs. Instantaneous reaction to seeing a man I once fancied I loved.'

'Fancied you loved? You were besotted by him, and he by you. Hell, I was only a kid, and I could feel the magic in the air whenever the two of you were together.'

'You were a very sweet kid, and you're an even nicer young man,' Sarah said, pressing a kiss on his cheek. 'But whatever we had ended a long time ago.'

'Then why did your body react so? Was it predictably or unpredictably?' James teased.

'Force of habit!' Sarah countered. 'It's how it remembered reacting whenever it saw him all those years ago. Put it down to early programming, like Pavlov's dogs.'

'Well, don't start panting,' James warned, craning to see above the crowd, 'because he's on his way. Doing it politely and stopping to chat, but moving inexorably towards you, lovely lady.'

Sarah closed her eyes and willed her body to behave, or for fate to swoop upon her and zap her into another time zone! When she opened them she was forced to admit James had been right. The dark head above an only slightly less dark suit was much closer now. Close enough for her to make out his craggy features—longish nose, strong jaw, high-set cheek-bones—and see more clearly where time had brushed his temples with those distinguished streaks.

Close enough now for her to hear his voice, deep and resonant—a parade-ground voice, he'd always said.

'Sarah!' Silver-grey eyes, as cool and clear as water, scanned her face, her body, then her face again, finally snagging her gaze and holding it.

'Tony.'

She nodded her head as he'd nodded to her earlier, and hoped he couldn't see the nerves jumping beneath her skin. Or realise the struggle she was having to stop her body flinging itself headlong into his arms and pressing hard against his muscled bulk.

'You're looking well.'

His voice spoke the words but his eyes were saying other things, teasing her to an even more heightened awareness of his presence, her trembling flesh reminding her of how it had been between them.

From their first meeting they'd shared a fiery physical attraction, although they'd restrained themselves, both wary in the face of such an all-consuming force, for at least a month!

'Politics isn't doing you any harm either,' she said, when she realised from the ongoing silence it was her turn to contribute.

He stepped closer and Sarah realised James had slipped away, his departure unnoticed once Tony had arrived.

The increased proximity escalated Sarah's tension and she moved instinctively backwards but found the bar blocking her retreat.

She stared at him, excited yet fearful, not wanting to lose again the control it had taken eleven long and lonely years to put in place. Could he read her ambivalence? See her aching hunger for his body? Know her mind was yelling warnings?

'I can't socialise right now. I have to stick with the boss in case he talks himself into difficulties and needs extricating. Where are you staying?'

He seemed so together—so unaffected by the whirlpool of emotions in which she was struggling—she made a superhuman effort to regain control.

'I'm at the cottage. I'm not here for the party. I'm working.'

'Working? At the hospital?'

Good! Now he seemed as flummoxed as she was.

'I'm a doctor. Where else would I be working?'

His head dipped as if to concede her the point in a game he was playing, then he said, 'How much longer will you be here?'

Now totally confused by the conversation, as well as her body's treachery, Sarah glanced at her watch.

'Not long. I came to drop Lucy off, and say hello, but, having blessed the McMurrays with my presence, I'll have to show up at the pub party.'

He grinned at her, causing further devastation to her nerves.

'Some things don't change in small country towns, but I wasn't asking about tonight. How much longer will you be in Windrush? How long's the locum?'

Unable to understand why he'd asked, she stared at him, and saw the silver eyes darken to a steely grey. She forced herself to breathe evenly, definitely not pant, for his eyes had darkened in just that way when they'd made love.

'A month. I've three more weeks,' she told him, biting off the question she'd have liked to have asked.

The smile this time was totally different—slow and seductive—but its effect was like a blowtorch as it scorched across her skin and sent more heat into her blood.

'And I've three days,' he said softly.

He reached out, lifted the half-finished glass of wine from her unresisting fingers and set it on the bar, then he grasped her shoulders, drew her close and kissed her firmly on the lips.

Before she had time to register either delight or protest he stopped—stepped back.

'Tomorrow,' he said, making the word a promise, then he wove his way back through the crowd to do his duty to the Minister.

Sarah waited until she could no longer see his head above the crowd, then, without a greeting or farewell to her host or hostess, she slipped quietly away, too disturbed— too excited—too darned confused—to talk to anyone.

CHAPTER TWO

'MUM, can you come? James is dead!'

Lucy's voice was unnaturally calm, but Sarah heard the click of disconnection before she could assimilate the news and begin to ask questions. In spite of her own sleep-drugged state, she realised it had taken a tremendous effort for her daughter to impart even that limited amount of information without hysteria.

Inside, she would be screaming her anguish—pain clawing at her intestines. Sarah knew this as well because she felt it herself, so strongly she had to remind herself that this was James, not David. This was now, not twenty years ago.

She squinted at the clock and worked out, if it really was six-fifteen, then she'd had plenty of sleep after fleeing the McMurrays' party, and stopping briefly at the pub.

Her body went into mechanical mode as her mind fired off the necessary orders. Get out of bed, into clothes, splash water on face, brush hair, clean teeth, no time for coffee, come on, you can do this, it happens all the time to doctors.

Listening to those orders rather than the whimpering of her heart, she drove swiftly towards Craigmoor, barely aware of the country through which she travelled, with its myriad shades of green and grey against the harsh red of the soil. Pain for Lucy mingled with her own sense of loss, but overriding all, for the moment, was the thought of what lay ahead for her professionally.

The law demanded documentation on all the milestones in a person's life—death not least among them. And young, healthy people didn't die naturally, so questions had to be asked and answered. Legally, by others—medically, by herself.

She suppressed a shudder at the thought of performing an autopsy on James, but knew her training and experience would enable her to do it efficiently and, she hoped, effectively.

A cloud of red dust ahead of her on the road told her someone else had been summoned. Presumably Ken Griffiths—uniformed representative of 'the law' in Windrush Sidings—a middle-aged man she'd met briefly earlier in the week.

Lucy was waiting on the drive, her face bleached white by shock and pain. Sarah held her close, and felt bones and skin and grief.

'Do you want to talk about it or not?' she asked. 'Would it help you cope, to tell me what you know?'

Lucy shook her head, but the words came tumbling out anyway.

'He was in the pool, drowned they say, lying on the bottom like a dark shadow of himself. Stewart says James was asleep out there when he and Alana went to bed. Stewart says he must have stumbled and fallen, maybe hit himself and knocked himself out, but I can't believe he'd do that. Not James... It's been dreadful, Mum. Alana kept prodding at Stewart with hints of James's moodiness and everyone knew she was suggesting suicide as a possible cause. Of course, Stewart refused to even consider such a thing—'

'And you? Would you consider it?' Sarah asked as the flow stopped too abruptly.

'No!' The despair in the word gave the lie to it, but then Lucy straightened slowly and stepped out of the comfort of her mother's clasp. She took a deep breath.

'A few years back I might have,' she said slowly. 'James was always obsessed by his mother's death—always puzzling over how it might have happened. He couldn't believe she'd have deliberately left him at such a dangerous time...'

'That's understandable. A death like that, with the question of suicide hanging over it! We feel more at ease when life is compartmentalised into tidy boxes—usually with lids that can be shut on the bits we don't want to remember. Not knowing exactly what happened to his mother—and why—must have tormented him.'

'Yes, but not lately. Since *Stop the Wheel Turning* sold he's been so positive. Working on a short, one-act play for the company in Sydney—absolutely brimming with life-force.'

Lucy's cheeks had regained some colour so Sarah, relieved by even such a small sign of normality, kept her talking.

'Brimming isn't quite the word I'd have used last night,' she said gently.

'Oh, Mum! You know how he dreads coming back to Craigmoor and "doing the dutiful" on Stewart's command. Dreads?'

Her face crumpled and she gave a little cry, then turned away, her shoulders slumped, to hide the tears coursing down her cheeks.

'I should have said "dreaded",' she mumbled into the handkerchief Sarah pressed between her fingers. 'How can I talk about James in the past tense?' she demanded, turning back to Sarah and casting her body into the waiting arms. 'How can I bear it?'

Sarah let her cry and then, as the sobs ceased, steered her daughter gently towards the car.

'Sit in there,' she ordered, opening the passenger door and helping Lucy in. 'I'll be as quick as I can, then drive you back to town. If you wait out here you won't have to see or talk to anyone.'

She walked away, feeling a familiar guilt as she remem-

bered other occasions when she'd known her daughter
needed her but work had compelled her to be elsewhere.

Was all of life a compromise?

'Philosophical meditation to stop you thinking about
James!' she muttered crossly to herself as she stepped onto
the low verandah. 'Great tribute to a young man you loved
almost as much as you love your daughter!'

She hesitated outside the front door as a tearing inside
her suggested philosophical debate was infinitely better
than feeling anything else at the moment. Later, she would
allow herself to feel all the grief and horror and sorrow and
regret churning in her intestines.

Later!

'The ambulance is on its way.' Ken Griffiths met her by
the door. 'The lad was in the pool and Stewart got him out.
Do you want to have a look here or wait 'til you get back
to town?'

'I'll have to see him,' Sarah replied, knowing she had
no choice. 'I'll check on Stewart and Alana as well while
I'm here, then I'd like to take Lucy back to town with me
when I go, if that's OK by you.'

Ken nodded.

'I've already spoken to her. The family have gone off to
their rooms and the overnight guests are in the living room.
Chris Barnes, Stewart's manager, has stayed with the body.
My constable is busy in town—processing a load of drunks
after the pub party last night.'

'What can I do to help?'

The words came out automatically. Although the title
was rarely used, she knew her job description included acting as the official Government Medical Officer in town, and
as such she would be involved in the investigation anyway.

'Would you sketch the area around the pool? I know
everything's a mess out there, but the coroner will have my
skin if I don't do what I can. Just make a note of where

those long chair things are and anything else that's lying around that he might have tripped on.'

Sarah shivered as she watched Ken open his notebook and tear out a couple of pages from the back.

She'd seen countless examples of the transience of life but could James have tripped and died *that* easily?

James?

Ken produced a pencil from his shirt pocket and handed it to her.

'Don't try to draw it to scale, but ask Chris to get the long tape from my truck, take measurements and jot them down. I can tidy it up later.'

'I've done it before,' Sarah assured him, and her mind wound back to another drowning not far from here, where she and Tony had worked in taut, strained silence, detailing the death of James's mother.

An image of the older Tony, as she'd seen him last night, presented itself in her mind and she had to force it away and concentrate on what had happened here.

The thought of James, as lithe and agile as a dancer, tripping and falling into the pool, doing sufficient damage to himself that he drowned, was…

Unbelievable?

Sarah shivered.

'I guess I'd better start asking questions,' Ken mumbled, discomfort radiating from him in almost visible waves as he fussily turned to a clean page. 'The problem in the country is that the people you question are usually friends as well as involved citizens, and as friends they tell you what they think you want to hear,' he added. 'Trying to help you do your job.'

'I don't envy you,' she said. 'I'll go and talk to Chris.'

Her stomach tightened and her breathing faltered as she headed for the courtyard. Such a narrow line between life and death, between everything and nothing…

James lay on his back, a soft tartan rug covering him as if to warm him as he slept.

'The boss couldn't bring himself to cover up his face,' Chris told her, and Sarah nodded, knowing she'd have hesitated, too.

'Ken's asked me to make a note of the area. Measurements and such, because there'll have to be an inquest. There's a long tape in his truck—could you get it then give me a hand?'

Chris sprang to his feet, obviously relieved his vigil was at an end.

'Will I bring back one of the boys to help?'

'Better not,' Sarah replied. 'I know things will have been moved already but the less we touch the better at the moment.'

Chris headed off, not through the house but skirting the old bedroom wing—he was help, not guest or family.

Sarah looked around.

The courtyard area had eight sun loungers, long white outdoor beds of slatted plastic with adjustable backs and wheels on one end so they could be moved easily.

She imagined they would normally be clustered companionably at the living-room end of the U-shaped courtyard, but some had obviously been moved. Pushed or pulled into pairs when guests had sought privacy last night? Or shoved aside when the alarm was raised and people came racing out of doorways to help—or watch?

On the tiles beneath or beside many of the loungers were cups and glasses. That in itself was unusual. Surely Alana, or one of her helpers, would have made a late sweep through the house, collecting up the dirty cups and glasses and stacking them into the dishwasher. There was nothing worse than facing the detritus of a party next morning.

'No suppositions!' she muttered to herself, as she stalked around the chairs, careful to disturb nothing. 'You're here, and responsible, and on the remote chance that something might be needed you will draw in all those innocent cups and glasses. You will drain their contents into little bottles then gather them up in evidence bags and number, seal and label each and every one of them.'

She frowned when she realised why she was being so adamant about it. Tony again! Was it because of last night's brief and tense reunion—not to mention the kiss—that today he seemed to be hovering over her shoulder like a poltergeist? Reminding her of things he'd said when she'd first worked with him on an accident scene.

'If we get the little things right in the beginning, Sarah, there'll be less confusion later,' he'd told her, and she'd tried to follow that rule ever since.

And had always thought of him as she'd gone through the motions.

No, she might have pretended she'd forgotten him, but he'd been too important in her life—too central to it for that short period of almost delirious bliss—for that to happen.

And now he was back.

Though not in her life.

Yet.

She closed her eyes for a moment, and reminded herself she was here to work, not think about the past. Dragging in a deep breath, she opened them to focus on the area around the tartan rug.

Damp towels lying scrunched up on the loungers suggested there'd been an attempt to dry—maybe to warm—James after he'd been lifted from the pool. Water lay in puddles on the tiles. More than one person had jumped in to attempt a rescue and had clambered out again with little regard for scientific evidence.

But despite this, Sarah felt compelled to search, to walk around the pool, studying the sharp edges of the heavy terracotta tiles which paved the courtyard. She knew it was a delaying tactic—something to do before she faced the reality of this much-loved young person's death. Knew also that she should be on her hands and knees with a magnifying glass if she was to find any evidence—a scraping of skin, a line of blood, a few hairs to show he'd hit his head as he'd gone into the blueness of the pool.

She could work that out from examining his head, common sense suggested, yet she continued her patrol of the perimeter, coming at last to a spot beside James's feet.

Water seeped from beneath the blanket, running in sluggish rivulets back towards the pool. She let her gaze travel up the length of his body, then finally settle on his face, turned towards the pool as if still seeking answers in the water—answers he would now never know.

Death was like the nothingness of sleep, yet in death the body altered in some way she had never been able to define, leaving vacant possession of the physical shell. But, as she continued to look, she noticed other changes.

His head had been deliberately turned to one side, no doubt by Stewart. The darkness of the livor mortis stains, caused by blood being drawn by gravity to the lower side as he lay face down in the pool, had been hidden from hasty but curious glances.

Sarah knelt beside the body and touched her fingers to the wet hair, said a silent goodbye to James, then switched from mourning friend to doctor.

There was a thin red mark, as precise as a ruled line, from the corner of his left eyebrow across his upper temple and running back into his hair. The skin was broken and a slight bruising coloured the area to either side. Had he fallen, hit his head and lost consciousness, then drowned before his body's defences reacted to the blow and left more of a mark?

Some bruising can occur after death...

She turned his head and pressed her fingers to the livid colour on his cheek. It blanched momentarily, and as she studied the crease of white along the bone she wondered

how immersion would affect any precise estimate of the
time of death.

'Oh, James!' she murmured softly, as tears blurred her
vision and grief betrayed her clinical approach.

Then, shamed by her momentary weakness, she lifted her
head and looked around. She couldn't bring James back to
life, but she was a professional. Her job was to find the
answers to satisfy both the coroner and the grieving family
and friends.

How and why. How first, she decided.

'Ambulance is here.'

Ken came out from the kitchen, his notebook still open
in one hand.

'I'll just bag his hands then they can take him,' she said,
touching the tartan rug with shaking fingers, then reaching
up to take two plastic bags from Ken. 'Tell them to bring
the ambulance around to the back.'

He disappeared from the doorway then returned a few
minutes later.

'You'll be quick with the sketch?'

It was half question, half order.

'I won't waste time,' she assured him. 'But it has to be
accurate. The coroner will have to decide if it was an accident or suicide. He'll need whatever help we can give
him.'

Ken shrugged uneasily.

'Mr McMurray's upset about the accident.' He stressed
the final word. 'He's worried about how more fuss will
affect the important guests. Naturally he'd like us out of
the way. He...'

Told you what to do and how to do it, Sarah finished
silently, but aloud she said, 'I'll be as quick as I can. I'll
draw in the position of the cups and glasses lying beside
the lounge chairs—it might help the guests remember who
was sitting where and when. We'll number them and take

them away...' She halted, knowing from his face she'd
overstepped some invisible boundary between them.

'But surely...'

Sarah could almost hear him wondering how he was going to explain such cavalier behaviour to Stewart—and
shuddering at the thought.

'He must have tripped and knocked himself out—they'd
all been drinking,' Ken protested.

All?

Sarah hesitated, aware how careful she must be. Aware,
too, that she would like it to be an accident because, in
some way, that would absolve her, as his friend, of any
responsibility.

But as he'd been a friend, didn't she owe him the truth?

'I know it's intrusive for Stewart and the family to have
us here, but if the lab finds traces of drugs in his blood
someone's going to ask where it came from and the first
thing they'll want to know is if it was in a drink.'

'And if I say we didn't look at the cups and glasses, I'll
be finishing my career before my next promotion,' Ken
agreed gloomily. He nodded for her to continue and walked
back into the house. She sketched quickly, numbering the
chairs, clumsily drawing in the relative positions of the
cups and glasses. Chris returned and she helped him measure, first the overall width of the area, keeping him busy
while the ambulance men removed the body.

'Walk back towards me, and measure from the kitchen
door, the sun-room door and the sitting-room door,' she
told Chris. These measurements could be done at any time
if they were needed, but getting them now meant Ken
wouldn't have to intrude again later. 'Then we'll do the
length of the bedroom wings and mark the doors that give
onto this area, then measure out to the pool on the three
sides.'

The ambulance attendants wheeled the trolley away. The
physical remains of James would be waiting for her when

she returned to town. Even in remote country areas these men saw enough death to know what was required.

Chris moved quickly, holding the free end of the tape wherever she pointed, waiting while she jotted down the measurement, then moving to the next spot, until she had all the figures Ken would need.

'Here's an evidence box, gloves on the top.' Ken returned as she was finishing. 'You can bag and tag those things you want, get Chris to sign as a witness and I'll do an authority for him later. Use the paper bags for the cups and glasses, moisture in the plastic ones causes problems. Some of the guests are anxious to leave, so I'll have to speak to them.'

She wanted to point out that the guests could wait a little longer, but she detected the firm hand of Stewart behind Ken's haste and simply nodded her agreement. As a government official she was expected to assist the police whenever and in whatever way might be required.

The bagging and tagging took another thirty minutes, then she left the courtyard, walking around the house to check on Lucy.

There was another car on the drive, a recent model Commodore in a dark olive green. And leaning back against it, with Lucy in his arms, was the man she'd been trying not to think about.

He nodded, again, this time over Lucy's head, then eased the girl away from his body. He must have said something for she turned towards Sarah.

'Uncle Tony says he'll find out what happened,' Lucy said. Her voice was stronger, as if Tony's promise had made everything easier for her to bear.

Stifling an impulsive, and definitely unworthy, spurt of jealousy that it was he making things right for *her* daughter, Sarah faced the man who had guided her through her first death scene.

'Officially?' she asked, hoping she sounded cooler than

she felt. 'Ken Griffiths is in charge here these days. He's inside now.' She hesitated and controlled an urge to run away, because her body, unheeding of the tragedy, was doing its reacting thing again.

But she'd stopped running away, she reminded herself.

And she'd loved James.

'Well?' she asked, more aggressively than she'd intended.

Silver grey eyes flicked across her face, while his remained impassive—unreadable.

'My boss insisted I come.'

'That's not an answer,' Sarah told him, as an angry heat supplanted the attraction's fire. 'Stewart's already told Ken it was an accident—that's all he wants to hear. What he wants Ken to find. And no doubt it's what your boss wants you to confirm for him.'

Sarah saw Lucy flinch at the anger in her voice. Tony tucked an arm around her daughter's shoulders and silenced her protest with a quickly whispered word.

'I will find out what happened to James,' he repeated, for Sarah's benefit this time. 'I don't make the same mistakes twice.'

He spoke quietly, without emphasis, but Sarah shivered as if an unfamiliar menace lurked beneath the words.

'Good,' she said, then turned her attention to Lucy. 'I won't be much longer, love, but I'd better see the family before I leave. I can't imagine Stewart admitting he might need a sedative, but Alana might appreciate something to help her sleep.'

She hurried away, wanting to get her daughter away from the place and needing to escape the man who comforted her.

Stewart must have seen her coming, for he emerged from the house to meet her on the verandah. Automatically, Sarah scanned his face, seeking signs of unendurable strain—signals that the body might be having difficulty functioning.

But Stewart's skin tone was clear, his colour no higher than usual, and his eyes clear and focussed.

Even his voice, when he spoke, was firm and strong.

'Thank you for coming. Is Lucy all right? She found him, you know. Found him and let out the most awful scream, then fainted. Alana tried to make her lie down but she wouldn't leave until we'd got him out of the pool.'

He spoke as if Lucy's reaction had been unnecessary, even distasteful, but Sarah's mind had flown off on another tack.

Was it Lucy who'd tried to dry him? Lucy who'd wanted 'normal' returned, and James to be alive?

Of course!

She swallowed hard and scrambled desperately back into her professional self.

'How are you feeling?' she asked Stewart. 'Physically, I mean? Do you want a sedative of some kind? Would that help?'

'Nothing will help,' he said firmly, then he sighed. 'We argued last night, James and I. About his so-called career.'

'For someone so young, he was doing very well in that so-called career.' Sarah automatically defended James.

'But Craigmoor was his destiny. How could he *not* have seen that?'

She heard the faint tremor in the words and realised Stewart wasn't as composed as he pretended. Was it grief she heard? Or anger that he hadn't been able to manipulate his son into a future he would now never have?

'What about Alana? Would you like me to see her, check her out?'

The master of Craigmoor waved his hand in a dismissive gesture.

'Alana already has enough pills and potions to open a

chemist's shop. She's sleeping at the moment, but I'll tell her to give you a call if there's anything you can do.'

The words strengthened Sarah's impression that her presence was no longer required—or welcome. Which suited her.

She turned away from him and walked towards the car, wondering if the unsteadiness in her knees was grief for James, reaction to Tony's continued presence on the scene or the lack of her morning caffeine boost.

'Have you had breakfast?' Tony demanded as soon as she was close enough to hear him. 'Coffee? Did they give you something at the house?'

She shook her head, thinking how familiar that scolding voice was, although she hadn't heard it for eleven years.

'I'll take Lucy home and get something there,' she assured him, because, unless he'd changed out of all recognition, he would keep nagging at her until he was satisfied she would look after herself.

'Well, see you do,' he said gruffly, his dark brows drawing together in so familiar a way she almost smiled. 'I'd come with you but I have to see Stewart. And this Griffiths fellow. Do what I can out here.'

He paused, then said, 'But I'll be back for the post. Don't start without me.'

Sarah saw Lucy flinch, then dart towards the car, heard Tony curse himself for upsetting her again, but uppermost in her mind was his final statement.

'Don't start without you?' she said. 'Why would you want to be there?'

He studied her for a moment then said, 'I told you, Sarah. I am going to find out what happened.' There was another pause, during which the metal-sheened eyes bored into hers. 'This time.'

And with that he strode away, leaving Sarah staring at his retreating back. As he came into focus as a person, rather than Tony, she realised he was back in his 'uniform'

of blue jeans and a dark checked shirt—far more familiar
to her than the man in the suit had been.

Not that she wanted familiar.

Did she?

CHAPTER THREE

THE question accompanied Sarah to the car.

Lucy acknowledged her with a nod, grudgingly pulled on her seat belt and snapped it fast, then folded her arms across her chest and stared out at the flat plains. Normally, the drive would have delighted Sarah, but today the surroundings were nothing more than a blur, her whole being concentrated on the pain radiating from Lucy's stiff body.

'It's the only way we'll find out what happened,' she said gently, forcing herself to say the words, to break the silence lying as thick as fog between them.

But she kept her eyes on the road, unable to bear the stricken look on her daughter's face.

'I must have fallen asleep!' Lucy said at last, the simple statement bearing such a load of guilt Sarah felt the car respond to her own startled reaction.

'I was in his room—waiting for him to come. We'd talked about the change in our relationship. He was wary about us—us having sex, and I guess I was pushing him a bit. We'd argued over such a silly thing, and I went to his room to apologise, although I suppose, if I'm totally honest, I wanted something to happen. It seemed right that we should start here at Windrush. I must have fallen asleep!'

Again the guilt! About falling asleep? Or wanting intimacy with the man she loved?

Surely not...

'I heard him come in, in the dark, fiddle with something on the lowboy as if he was getting undressed, taking things out of his pockets first, but I must have drifted off again. When I woke it was daylight and he wasn't there. I don't

37

know why I went out to the pool—except that he'd been there when I left him. Oh, Mum!'

The grief and tears came pouring out. Sarah eased the car onto the verge and stopped. She undid her seat belt, reached across to release Lucy's, then put her arms around her daughter's shaking shoulders and drew her close.

'We'd argued over a cup of coffee, of all things,' Lucy muttered. 'A bloody cup of coffee, and it meant I didn't have a chance to say goodbye!'

'It probably wasn't the coffee so much as the tension of visiting Craigmoor. You'd both been under a strain,' Sarah comforted.

'But I'll remember the coffee!' Lucy wailed. 'A stinking dirty cup of coffee he was holding in his hand. I said I'd like a cup, expecting him to pass it to me because we both drink it black with sugar. He went on and on about it not being a cup of coffee but something different—a symbol. He made out it was the first little bit of personal attention his father had ever shown him. You know what James was like, Mum, arguing in that infuriatingly semantic way he had. Sheesh, I argue often enough myself over ridiculous things, but a cup of coffee?'

Sarah could feel Lucy's remembered anger jostling with her grief, and knew exactly what she meant. She'd been arguing with David, Lucy's father, the last time they'd been together, before he, too, had died prematurely. Killed in a car accident. Even after twenty years regrets still lingered.

'So you told him what to do with his cup of coffee and stormed off,' she said softly, imagining the scene.

'Then went to sleep! What if he came in to go to bed but saw I was sleeping and decided not to disturb me…'

Again such anguish. She knew Lucy was picturing James, seeing in her mind his silent retreat from the room, a careless step by the pool, falling…

'Those old rooms are very dark,' Sarah reminded her, thinking of a night she'd once spent at Craigmoor. 'If he didn't turn on the light he wouldn't have realised you were there. He might have come in for any reason, then left again.'

But Lucy wasn't going to be comforted that easily.

'I should have called to him, made him talk to me, kept him by me. After all, I persuaded him to go home. It was my fault he was there.'

'You couldn't have sat watching him all night,' Sarah pointed out. 'He was a grown man, Lucy. He didn't need protection. And as you said, he was on top of the world. There was no reason to fear for him,'

'But if I hadn't argued... If I'd stayed and we'd talked a while, then gone into bed together—surely that would have made a difference, Mum.'

'There are so many ''ifs'', love, so many variables. Believing it's preordained is easier than wondering what might have been.'

She smoothed the pale, fair skin on her daughter's arms, and felt the warm, wet tears soaking through her shirt. Lucy's muscles were relaxing, the tension of anger and despair washing out of her, allowing grief to hold sway at last.

'I'm OK now!' she mumbled after a few more minutes, and she drew away, no longer a child, seeking comfort in her mother's arms, but a young woman again.

Sarah didn't argue. She started the car and drove slowly back to town, holding her own pain—for Lucy, and for James—in check.

'I've got to go across to the hospital,' she said when Lucy had refused tea, coffee or sedation of any kind and had curled into a foetal ball on the spare bed in the meagrely furnished doctor's quarters.

Lucy nodded, and Sarah knew she'd withdrawn again, locking herself back into her misery—at least partially to escape the thought of why her mother had to go over to the hospital.

Sarah drew on all her reserves of professionalism. She found the soft mohair travel rug she always carried with her, and folded it around Lucy's legs and shoulders, then walked away from her daughter's pain, knowing she couldn't take it from her—or bear it for her.

Graham Logan was waiting at the morgue. He'd been an established orderly at the hospital when she first came to Windrush Sidings and was close to retirement now. Calm and deliberate of movement, slow of speech, he somehow fitted the city-dweller's image of a man born and reared in the country. But to Sarah he was a welcome sight, someone she could trust to help her without unnecessary fuss or ribald comments.

'I've done the photographs and weighed and measured him,' he said quietly, as she donned a gown and changed from shoes to plastic boots. 'Wrote it down for you. Took a handkerchief, a pen and a little notebook out of his pockets and wrote them down, too. Bad business, this. The Boss must be upset.'

'The Boss' meant only one person in this area, but Sarah wondered if he *was* upset. Controlled and wary, certainly. Perhaps angry. But upset?

'I can't start until—'

'Ken want to be here?' Graham guessed.

'Possibly, although he didn't mention it.'

Sarah stopped, uncertain how to go on, knowing whatever she said was going to spring the lid on a past she didn't want to review.

'You know Ned Burrows is guest of honour for the celebrations?'

'Drumming up support for the next election, more like.'

'Tony Kemp's with him.' Sarah blurted out the words.

'Guess I already knew that.' Graham could take laconic to extremes. 'Someone must have said. He the one who wants to be here?'

Sarah nodded.

'Good thing, then,' Graham decreed. 'He should have been here for the first one.'

'Do you mean that?' Sarah demanded. She was puzzled, not by his reference to the 'first one', correctly identifying that as James's mother, but because she'd thought the town had all been on Stewart's side back then. She'd assumed his pulling strings to get rid of Tony so quickly had been approved, and possibly applauded.

'I've never believed that man did half the things the town got to saying he did. Far as I could see, he was so taken up with you at the time I doubt he knew any other women existed.'

Sarah stared at the older man. First James and now Graham—remembering Tony's love for her the way she'd thought it had been.

Until…

'You didn't say that at the time,' she told Graham.

'You weren't listening at the time,' a deep voice said, and she turned to find Tony in the doorway. He stepped forward, towards Graham not her, greeting the older man with a handshake and a quick slap on the shoulder. 'Are you ready to start?'

The question was addressed to her, and, although she knew she'd never be ready, she turned towards the table, Tony's presence unwittingly strengthening her for the task ahead.

She looked at James—but knew it wasn't James. His body perhaps, but not the young person she'd loved.

'We could send him to town,' Tony suggested, as if he'd read her regrets in her face.

'Town' was an hour and half away by road, and had a larger hospital to suit its five-thousand population.

But the doctors in town hadn't known James.

Wouldn't have cared!

'No, it's my job. I'll do it,' she said, snapping on her gloves and studying the still form.

James's clothes were drying, patchy dark and damp at groin and armpit, crumpled dry across his chest, the zip of his jeans a darker, less faded blue. The plastic bags on his hands looked grotesque so she slipped them off, then lifted the lifeless fingers of his right hand first.

She'd insisted they collect and tag all the cups and glasses by the pool. Having done that, she'd need James's prints for comparison. She hesitated, knowing they could probably be lifted from a dozen places—his car, his bedroom at the house—then made up her mind.

'We'll print him just in case,' she said, then, as Graham handed her slides, she pressed first his thumb, and then his fingers onto the glass surfaces, wondering if immersion, even for a short time, altered the oil in the skin that helped produce clear prints.

'Label each one,' she said to Graham, although she knew he'd do it properly.

She moved on to examine the skin of the hands, and particularly his nails. Had he flailed out, tried to grab the edge, torn his skin, caught a fingernail on the tiles?

'He didn't struggle?'

Tony asked the question and she shook her head, although she took nail scrapings for analysis to be sure.

'People who drown usually do,' she said, 'unless...'

'Don't guess,' Tony warned. 'Stick to facts, not suppositions.'

His voice was somehow new to her, as if her ears had to relearn its notes, yet familiar enough to be reassuring.

'Ready?' Graham switched on the tape and it whirred softly, reminding her of the job. She began to speak to the machine. Skin tone—lividity marked but not fixed, the redness bleaching to white when she pressed a finger to it, absence of surface lesions—scratches or bruises—on fingers, hands, arms.

Next she set a piece of plastic beneath his head and

combed his hair, then dropped the plastic and the comb into a bag Graham held for her.

'Thorough,' Tony commented, in such a flat voice Sarah had no idea whether he approved or disapproved.

'It's habit,' she told him, although she knew it wasn't normally done unless murder was suspected or the victim's identity was unknown.

So?

Silently apologising to the James she'd known for the intrusion, she drew a little fluid from his left eye and dispensed it into a tube for labelling, then injected in the equivalent amount of water to prevent the eye looking too sunken. These days vitreous fluid could be used to gauge time of death more accurately than rigor, but with immersion it might be different. So much fluid involved!

She cursed herself for not knowing more—reading the latest professional magazines wasn't always enough—and concentrated on the next step.

'We'll take off his shoes first,' she said, turning from the microphone. Tony came forward and examined the shoes, then pointed to the elasticised sides and suggested Graham cut through there. Tony hovered, watching closely, pulling on gloves himself to take the shoes as Graham removed them, studying them again before setting them on the bench to be bagged later.

Sarah waited until the men were done, then stripped off the damp socks and felt the coldness of those lifeless toes. She wanted to wail like a banshee, howling out her frustration that death could cheat her—cheat her daughter— like this.

'Hard for an adult to drown in a pool.'

Graham's flatly delivered statement brought her out of her thoughts. She glanced at Tony, half expecting him to reprimand Graham for conjecture.

He was wearing his policeman's face—expressionless—

and Sarah wondered again just why he was here. Then he spoke.

'Damned hard for an adult to drown in a pool!' he said softly, and her heart lifted. Perhaps he did intend to keep his promise to Lucy. He *would* work out what had happened, so at least she'd know!

She refocussed on her work, helping Graham cut away James's clothes, setting them aside to be bagged and labelled later. Again they weighed and photographed the body, then she began a new examination, head to toes, front and back, seeking bruises, cuts, wounds of any kind, searching for a clue as to what had happened in the dark, lonely hours of the night.

It was a standard procedure, carried out so often during the years she'd spent in one-doctor towns which were so far from large hospitals it made shifting bodies impractical. It's not James, it's a corpse, she told herself, and proceeded with her external examination, taking samples and dictating as she went, measuring the length and describing the colour of the mark across his temple—taking more photographs.

She pressed her hand hard against his chest and saw pink-tinged foam appear on his lips and around his nose.

'Does that mean he inhaled water into his lungs? That he was alive when he went into the pool?' Tony asked, stepping close again, his presence both a comfort and a distraction.

'It could be pulmonary oedema—fluid collected in the lungs from the blood, not the swimming pool,' she warned. 'Facts, not suppositions,' she reminded him.

She felt the clammy jaw and neck for rigor and noted down her findings.

'Does being immersed alter the timing of rigor setting in?' Again it was Tony asking questions.

Sarah thought back to her training days.

'I'd have to check it out to be one hundred per cent certain, but I know that if a person drowns by accident, but was conscious and fought to stay alive, rigor sets in very quickly as the body's reserves are depleted by the struggle. But an unconscious body is a different matter, and on top of that there's the water temperature. Damn, I didn't think to take it. Presumably the pool is heated.'

'We can do it later,' Tony assured her. 'If the pool's heated it will be on a thermostat, so the temperature should be fairly constant.' Then, in a transition so smooth it startled her, he said, 'Why would you think he might not have been conscious?'

'Because, as you and Graham have both remarked, it's damned hard for an adult to drown in a pool.'

She pointed to the abrasion, and frowned at her thoughts.

Tony voiced them for her as he bent to take a closer look

'Would a bump so light it left only redness and slight bruising knock a grown man unconscious?'

'It's on his temple, so possibly,' she said, but it didn't sit easily with her. Any more than the thought of James falling and striking his head made sense.

Although it was more believable than suicide.

'Ready?' Graham prompted, and Sarah, after another long look at the slim young figure, donned more layers of protective gear and pulled on the fine metal mesh gloves she used for handling the saws, then plastic gloves over them. She began the first incision.

Blood first. She found the jugular vein. Had someone said he'd been drinking? Graham passed her a number of sterile phials which she filled with the uncontaminated blood.

She cut further and waited for the lungs, suffused by water in most drownings, to balloon out. It didn't happen. Because they weren't suffused by water. Nor were they pale and wet-looking. They were pinkish, and certainly not heavy.

'He didn't drown?'

Tony was jumping to conclusions again in spite of his warning to her.

'A drowning can show either a great deal of water in the lungs, particularly if the victim took a long time to drown, or it can show almost none,' she told him, but she was puzzling over it herself. 'There are two types of drowning, wet and dry. The dry is caused by a spasm of the larynx, effectively choking the victim to death. Or a victim can die from a reflex cardiac arrest caused by sudden immersion in water, but that isn't actually drowning.'

She didn't add that the latter usually occurred when a heavily intoxicated person fell into water because she couldn't bring herself to believe James had been drinking.

James's drug of choice had been marijuana, not alcohol, and he used it only rarely, a social gesture of belonging.

'Will you be able to tell exactly what happened?' Tony asked.

'Probably not,' she told him. 'Drownings are the hardest of all deaths to classify successfully. And as the heart always stops beating when a person dies, it's impossible to say if that happened before or after he went into the water. With wounds it's easier because blood loss helps you determine if the heart was pumping at the time the wound was inflicted. But drowning?'

She shrugged off her frustration.

'What about pool chlorine? Could that be found in the fluid from his lungs?'

Sarah frowned at him.

'He was in the pool so presumably that's where he drowned—if he drowned—so that's not an issue. I mean, it's hardly likely someone drowned a fully clothed young man in the bath then shifted him to the pool under the noses of who knows how many house guests.'

He half smiled at her and her body responded as swiftly as if he'd stuck her with a pin. It reminded her of the previous evening, of joking with James about reactions...

Sweet heaven, she had to stop remembering.

'I hadn't considered bath water,' Tony told her. 'I was wondering whether traces of chlorine would show that at least some of the water present in his lungs had been inhaled.'

Chlorine?

She considered it for a moment.

'I'll ask the lab to check but I'm pretty sure chlorine dissipates too quickly for traces to be found.'

She turned her attention back to the lungs, describing their appearance in clinical terms. The small haemorrhages usually present in deaths where lack of oxygen was a factor were evident, but weren't as numerous as she'd have expected in a drowning. It added to her instinctive impression that James hadn't struggled, had perhaps been deeply unconscious or close to death when he'd entered the water. Which meant the knock on the head had been harder than it looked.

If he'd fallen—

Stop guessing.

With finicky care she took more blood, this time from the heart, then aspirated fluid from the lungs and bottled and labelled it, followed by more fluid from the bladder—traces of drugs were usually found in urine.

It's not James, she kept reminding herself, but when it came time to lift and weigh the organs her own heart began to thud unevenly. Behind her Tony moved, and she felt his hand touch her lightly on the shoulder.

'You can do it,' he said gently, and she blinked back a tear and set her mind on autopilot.

Heart and lungs, trachea—describe, weigh, pack them for despatch to the city labs. She recited the contents of each container, time and date into the machine, information for the labels she would attach later.

Liver, spleen, stomach—weigh, take samples of the contents, resections. It was work she let her fingers do while

her mind asked why she hadn't said it was an accident and
performed a limited autopsy. The mark on his face and the
small amount of fluid in the lungs would have justified it.
Wouldn't it?

Of course not.

Not for James.

Or for Lucy.

An image of the pair as she'd seen them only yesterday
drove her on, completing the full medical and legal autopsy—nothing but the best for James.

Only it's not James, she repeated to herself as she peeled
back skin to expose his skull. She had to see if there'd been
any sudden perfusion of blood in his brain—if the outer
sign of a head injury had minimised the damage.

Grown men didn't drown in pools!

He'd been so happy—delighted with the success of his
play, beginning to be confident of his future direction.
Happy people didn't kill themselves.

So there'd be blood, signs that the crack on his head,
however it had happened, had been worse than it looked
on the outside—bad enough to have knocked him senseless.

Yet still she hesitated—wanting proof of some kind, a
certainty—reluctant to desecrate the face she knew so well.

She took the next step, her fingers shaking now.

'He could have been knocked out, unconscious from a
fall perhaps. I should be able to tell,' she muttered to the
men who watched her work. She was trying to convince
herself, not them, trying to find the impetus for the next
move in this macabre sequence of events.

Saw through the skull. You've done it often—it's a body
not a person.

But tears splashed on the saw, and her voice was choked
as she described what she saw. Clean, glistening grey-white
hemispheres of the brain—a few pinpoint petechiae, but no
clots, no haematomas, no dark patches to show the injury
had rendered him unconscious.

'He was a nice youngster,' Graham said. 'Always kind to other kids. Took to my grandson, Edward, and looked after him at school.'

'My Lucy, too,' Sarah whispered, accepting Graham's tribute to the dead. And once again she felt a slight pressure on her shoulder—Tony's touch—of understanding this time.

She blinked away fresh tears and tried to think logically. There didn't have to be physical signs of concussion, her head was saying, but her heart was hammering at her rib-cage like an out-of-kilter top.

If he didn't drown and wasn't knocked unconscious...

She noted her findings, hearing the hoarseness of the unacknowledged dread in her voice and hoping the men would attribute it to her grief.

Then slowly and carefully she closed the incision. It took time, but it was the last thing she could do for James—well, that and find out how he'd died.

When all the test results came back...

'I'll clean up here, Graham,' she said quietly. 'Isn't today your day off? You'll want to join the festivities.'

He nodded.

'I'm not that keen on partying these days,' he said as he finished cleaning down the table and covered the body with a white sheet. 'When I heard about this happening, I figured I'd be the best one to help you do it. I thought a lot of the lad when he was younger.'

Sarah swallowed the lump in her throat and nodded to the older man.

'You want me to do the parcels?' he asked. 'I don't mind.'

Do the parcels! Packaging and labelling samples and specimens, sending off bits of James so men in white coats could tell her what he'd eaten and whether there were any abnormalities in his blood or tissues that might have made him pass out and fall into the pool.

'No, I'll do it, Graham,' she replied. 'I'll run the tape and write the labels from it. You could phone Dick Wells and organise for him to take the body.'

He nodded agreement and she waited while he wheeled the body into the small cooled room where it would wait until the mortician arrived to collect it. Then she turned to Tony and really looked at him for the first time since he'd walked into the room. He was as pale as she felt, his face older than her memories of it, more laugh lines teasing out from the corner of his eyes and a faint scoring down each cheek.

Yet in spite of the differences he was as familiar to her heart as her own reflection was to her eyes, and she ached for all they'd lost.

That other time.

'Do you want to check on Lucy?' he asked.

She hauled her mind back from maudlin sentimentality as suspicion once again waved flags in her head.

'I should,' she said, but stood her ground.

He guessed her thoughts and stepped towards her, grasping her shoulders and looking deep into her eyes.

'I, too, loved James,' he reminded her, 'and even without that incentive I owe Stewart McMurray.'

'For sending you away? Getting you a promotion as a reward for keeping quiet about your affair with his wife?' Sarah flung at him as something inside her snapped. 'Putting you on the fast track to success so you can be a flunkey to a government minister? For all of that you'll repay him by saying this is an accident and staying here to do what? Contaminate samples so nothing can be proved—'

His fingers tightened so the mesh of the metal vest she wore beneath her plastic gown bit into her shoulders, the pain stopping her flow of angry words.

'For sending me away, yes. For destroying my relationship with you by all but confirming those stories with his action in getting rid of me. You wouldn't listen then, Sarah.

I hope like hell you're listening now because this isn't over by a long shot.' He paused and she saw the glint of anger fade from his eyes, then the colour deepen as he added, 'And nor are we!'

He leaned towards her and she thought he was going to kiss her again. Her skin prickled, and her heart beat harder, sending blood flushing through her body. But as suddenly as it had started it stopped. He released her and stepped back, putting space between them.

Cold space.

'I'll check on Lucy, and then I'll be right back.' The smile he threw her mocked and taunted. 'See, Sarah, I have more trust in you than you do in me! But, then, I always did!'

He walked away, leaving her staring after him, confused by the sudden flare of emotion between them. And by his anger and the overtones of bitterness she'd heard beneath it.

She stripped off her gloves, then the extra layers of clothes until she was down to a lab coat. She washed her hands then dried them carefully and rewound the tape, before drawing on clean gloves.

Stalled.

What had he meant when he'd said she hadn't listened? Heaven knew, her ears had ached with listening while her heart had cracked open with the strain of what she'd heard. It had been all over town. Tales of Anna McMurray's visits to the police station—to the station house, usually after dark.

Tony's version of it had been that Anna hadn't been well, that she'd suspected someone was poisoning her. She'd come clandestinely because she'd been afraid. But Sarah had been her friend, and for Anna not to have come to see her professionally—not to have mentioned being unwell—had made the story thin to say the least! Hard to believe.

Then at the peak of the floods, when all the men in town

and most of the women were raising levee banks and shifting stock, Anna McMurray had disappeared.

That's in the past—not connected with what happened here, Sarah reminded herself. This is James, not Anna.

Yet the image of Anna's body when they'd found it, bloated and misshapen, torn by the buffeting in flood waters, rose in Sarah's mind and she had to fold her arms across her stomach to prevent herself being ill.

'She's sleeping.'

Tony's voice jerked her back to the present, but even so she stared blankly at him for a moment as she made the mental leap from then to now.

'Did you suspect foul play with Anna?' she asked him, remembering how meticulously he'd detailed the death scene. 'Is that what you meant about Stewart sending you away?'

'Once he'd had me ordered out of town there was no one to conduct an investigation,' he pointed out. 'Did you do an autopsy?'

Sarah shook her head.

'A token gesture,' she admitted. 'After we'd finished at the scene I came back to town, expecting Dick Wells to bring the body to the hospital. I was flat out in Cas at the time, so many people coming in with minor injuries they'd ignored for days because they were too busy fighting flood waters. Most of the wounds had turned septic and had to be cleaned out, a couple of people had mild cases of pneumonia. It wasn't until I finished work in the early hours of the morning that I realised it hadn't arrived.'

'And?' His eyes were locked on her face, but they hid his thoughts too well for her to guess where this was going.

'I went to bed,' she said flatly, remembering the physical and emotional exhaustion she'd carried with her that night. 'I intended to ask you next morning what I should do, but you'd gone by the time I phoned. I rang Dick instead. He said he'd been told to take her straight to the funeral home.

He'd already started work, replaced blood with embalming fluid. He said he was trying to make her look more human than when we'd seen her.'

'Why?'

The second single-word question hit her like a rock.

'Why?' she echoed, puzzled by his intensity. 'Why did he want her to look better? Perhaps for James? He was only young—about ten. Do you suppose Stewart suggested James might like to see her?'

Tony dismissed her feeble suppositions with an impatient wave of his hand.

'Why embalm her? What would have been the normal procedure for death even then? A closed coffin and cremation surely?'

She smiled at him.

'In Windrush Sidings? If you want cremation you have to die in Karunga or get your relatives to cough up for a three-hour round trip for Dick Wells to take you into town. Anyway, even with cremation, the body still needs preparation. Fluids drained—'

He held up his hand to stop the explanation.

'I don't want a lecture on what will happen to my body when I go,' he told her. 'I want to know what happened to Anna.'

The demand made Sarah's heart feel heavy with remembered sorrow.

'To her body.'

'To her body?'

He sighed impatiently.

'Get with it, Sarah. This could be important, and who knows how long we'll have before someone else arrives to pass on Stewart's latest edict?'

'You want to know where Anna's buried?' The heaviness intensified. 'I assume in the family plot on Craigmoor. Apparently there was once a church out there and it's consecrated ground. All the McMurrays, from when time be-

gan for white people out here, are buried there.' She
thought of James—Anna and heavy hearts forgotten as her
sorrow returned.

'We could have her exhumed!' he muttered, the words
said more to himself than to her so it took her a while to
work out what he'd said—let alone grasp the meaning.

'Exhumed?'

He stepped towards her and clapped a hand across her
mouth so quickly she went rigid with shock, then almost
limp with other feelings as his body pressed against hers
and he held her to him.

'Don't say anything out loud, or to anyone but me,' he
whispered. Although it had been a warning, the words held
tenderness as well.

Not that there was time to think about tenderness.

'You can't suspect Stewart McMurray of murdering his
son!' she hissed at him.

'Why not?' Tony said gruffly. 'I've always suspected he
got rid of Anna.'

Sarah was glad of his strong grip, for her knees had gone
weak at the verbal expression of her own inner, but unacknowledged fears.

'But he's next to God out here,' she muttered, while she
tried to get her knees to behave and her feet to move her
away from the warmth of Tony's strong, muscled body.

'Exactly. And if he's started to believe his own publicity,
it could be very easy for him to slip into the major role.'

He let her go, but kept one hand on her shoulder, steady-
ing her perhaps.

'Playing God?'

She was glad of the hand, for the shiver of fear began
in her toes and worked its way upward, while an icy dread
rustled like a wintry wind along her nerves.

'Playing God!' Tony confirmed.

CHAPTER FOUR

SARAH couldn't grasp the idea—not all at once—so sought escape in work.

'I have to finish up here. There's so much to do.'

She waved her hand towards the samples, packages and bottles on the bench. Better to keep busy. That way she wouldn't have time to think. She opened the cupboard and withdrew what she'd need—evidence bags and tags, packaging for liquids and soft, squashy, decomposing tissues, seals and labels. It was part of her job, although today no easier for all the practice she'd had over the years.

But no amount of fussing could stop her brain picking at the idea Tony had offered it.

'Why?' she asked. 'Aren't the police strong on motive? Why would he kill either of them?'

She packed, bottled and labelled as she spoke, and as she waited for Tony to reply.

First he checked the tape recorder, then, as if to ensure it couldn't secretly and malevolently record his words, he slipped the batteries out of it.

'Going to check for bugs?' she suggested, glancing around the laboratory-like room.

He chuckled and then shrugged as if to make light of such paranoia, but she sensed he was uneasy. Which didn't help the prickliness in *her* skin!

'He married Alana not long after Anna's death,' he pointed out.

'That was convenient,' Sarah suggested. 'After all, she was there, wasn't she? Anna's cousin, his own vague relation, already living with them to help Anna with the house, with James.'

'Was Anna sickly?' Tony asked. 'When you first knew her? I mean, having Alana living with them was strange, wasn't it?'

Sarah puzzled over the questions, ignoring a leap of joy that he should ask—as if he *hadn't* known Anna all that well.

'I think it was accepted in most country homes that someone would live in as help. According to James, they'd had a cook-housekeeper originally. Not the range of servants Stewart's forefathers would have had, but more help than city people would have considered normal.'

'More help than they've got now,' Tony pointed out. 'Kathy Barnes was serving savouries last night but she'd only been called in for the night.'

'Alana prides herself on her organisational skills,' Sarah told him. 'Lucy and James often joked about it. Apparently, when the cook-housekeeper left, Alana took on everything.'

'I remember the cook—she had a flower name of some kind. She often took pity on a poor single cop and would bring in casseroles when she came to town. No doubt Stewart paid for the ingredients, but she was a terrific cook. I wonder if she's still in Windrush?'

Sarah shook her head.

'I know James had lost touch with her and regretted it, so she must have moved away.'

'I wonder where she went. And why,' Tony murmured, almost to himself.

But Sarah heard, and felt another shiver of fear.

'Have you finished? Does it all go to town?'

Tony's question diverted her mind back to the present.

'No. I keep duplicate samples here. In fact, depending on what test kits are available here, I may be able to do some simple tests on his blood.'

'For alcohol?'

'That's easy. The police often require those so there should be a kit for that.'

'And drugs?'

She hesitated. In her mind, now that she'd ruled out concussion, the only way James could have gone into the pool was if he'd been drunk or drugged, but she wasn't an expert at forensic work. Although colour tests for simple things like barbiturates and opium based drugs were easy to perform, she didn't know if running tests here might muddy the waters if her results and the lab's didn't correspond.

'I'll test for alcohol because that changes with time, and I'll keep the samples, but—'

'Would barbiturates be the most likely? Some common prescription drug?'

'Barbiturates aren't so common these days. They've mostly been replaced by the benzodiazepine family, although people who need more heavy-duty sedation for whatever reason could still be prescribed barbiturates.'

She answered him absent-mindedly, her mind more concerned with drug tests.

The test for barbiturates was simple, using a chemical reagent that turned a purplish blue in the presence of barbiturates, but her doubts remained...

She left her packaging and turned to face him, looking into his eyes.

'If I go ahead and do a test, then I'm called to take the stand at an inquest, my credentials would be laughed out of court. Not to mention conflict of interest because, like it or not, Lucy's involved here. It's better to let the experts do it. That way there can't be any argument.'

He reached out and touched her gently on the cheek.

'You're right. I'm sorry for pressuring you like that when you've been through so much. Now, what can I do to help?'

She'd warmed at that touch, and to the gentleness in his voice as he'd apologised, but the offer of help put her back on edge.

'You can stand clear until I finish,' she said. 'That way there's no contamination of the evidence.'

Ken Griffiths arrived as she was sealing the last pack, pressing the Forensic Institute's sticky address label onto the outside. He glanced at the neat collection of cool-boxes with their warning signs asking that they be kept refrigerated and handled with care.

'That looks like a lot of samples. Did you do a full autopsy?' he asked.

'It seemed like a good idea,' Sarah replied, although from the look on Ken's face he wasn't in total agreement.

'You been here throughout?' he asked Tony.

'You want me to sign the chain of evidence statement?' Tony countered.

'Well, I can't, can I?' Ken muttered.

His obvious uneasiness made Sarah feel uncomfortable, but Tony pushed her to one side and began to sign the forms she'd completed, then initial the taped seals on all the boxes.

Ken watched, his face expressionless, then he said, 'I'm going to lift the prints off the cups and glasses next,' he said. 'I'll set them on cards and keep them filed at the station. I can take prints out at the house to match up with them if that happens to prove necessary later on.'

He spoke with more assurance this time, letting Sarah know that, although he'd gone along with her quaint idea to remove Stewart McMurray's personal possessions, he was now back in charge and running the investigation his way.

'Will you send this stuff or will I?' Sarah asked, waving to the carefully packed cool-boxes. He hesitated for a moment and she wondered if he wasn't as much in control as he made out. If he, too, had felt a tingle of uncertainty.

'It'll kill the Boss if the coroner finds suicide,' he muttered, answering her unspoken question if not the one she'd asked.

'I doubt it,' Sarah replied. 'Stewart McMurray's harder than the country hereabouts, and that's saying something.

Besides, with drowning, unless there's a suicide note, the verdict usually comes in as accidental death.'

She kept quiet about her own niggling misgivings. Let Tony tell his colleague if he wanted a more sinister issue raised. Not that Ken was likely to believe their 'playing God' theory.

Ken hesitated for a moment, then shrugged as if to dismiss his own reservations. He turned to Tony.

'Are you official here or what?'

'As official as an order from the Police Minister can make me,' Tony told him, and Sarah saw Ken relax.

'Would you come over to the station while I do the prints? I need a witness's signature on the cards and I don't want the young fellow knowing too much about what's going on. He's a good lad, but you know how talk gets around.' He glanced at Sarah. 'You could come, too.'

As an olive branch it wasn't bad, Sarah decided.

'I'll go across to the house and check on Lucy first,' she told him. 'Will you take the boxes?'

'Guess so! I'll drive them into town myself when we've finished at the office. Put them on this afternoon's flight to the city.'

'The bag to one side has the slides with James's fingerprints. If you're printing the cups and glasses you'll need them.'

Ken sighed as if he'd reached his limit of being told what to do, but checked the bag and signed the tag to officially take charge of the slides.

Sarah felt relieved. In spite of his reluctance to consider suicide earlier, he was showing all the signs of being a 'by the book' cop—not a bad thing in a small town where everyone knew everyone else and it was easy to edge the rules a little bit this way or that.

'I'll see you shortly,' she told the two men as they carried their load to the car. 'If Lucy's all right.'

But they got no further than the police car for Stewart

McMurray's tan Range Rover pulled up, effectively blocking the exit. Sarah moved instinctively, edging closer to Tony who steadied her with a swift touch on her elbow.

'Alana tells me you took cups and glasses from my house,' the big man stormed as he strode towards them. He directed his words at Ken but Sarah flinched as if his anger was aimed directly at her. 'What's the idea of it?'

He glared at Tony.

'Did you sanction it?' he demanded wrathfully. 'I thought you were asked to help!'

'I knew nothing about it,' Tony said, and this time Sarah flinched for another reason, though a firmer pressure on her elbow warned her to keep quiet. 'However, I can understand Ken wanting to follow the correct procedure,' he added. 'You don't want questions asked later.'

'What questions could possibly be asked? The lad slipped, hit his head and drowned. It was that simple. Isn't it enough I've lost my only son, without you people making a grand production of it? Boosting your own egos with an over-the- top investigation!'

Again Tony became the focus of his anger.

'I specifically asked Ned to see you handled this with finesse, not great clod-hopping police boots! Seems you haven't learned much in eleven years, for all the highfaluting degrees and titles you've amassed.'

No wonder Ken had been tentative, Sarah thought, seeing a side of the charming Stewart McMurray she'd never seen before. Guessing both men were now tongue-tied, she stepped into the breach.

'I think it's best to go by the rules in difficult situations,' she said carefully. 'We've done that!'

Stewart scowled at her.

'You're a fine one to talk about rules,' he growled, stepping closer and leaning aggressively towards Sarah. 'You and that daughter of yours. Encouraging that writing non-

sense of his, seducing him from his family. This whole
thing's her fault!'

Tony caught Sarah by the arm before she could react.

'You're overwrought,' he said to Stewart, his voice cold
enough to cool even Sarah's over-heated blood. 'We'll
grant you the excuse of grief, but I think it's time you
returned home and dealt with your suffering there, instead
of taking it out on people who are trying to help you.'

'I want my belongings returned,' he roared, his face red-
dening so much Sarah forgot her anger to worry about his
health.

'When we've finished with them I'll personally see to
it,' Tony told him. He stepped forward, tucking Sarah behind him, and straightened to his full height, squaring his
shoulders and somehow giving off an air of quiet deter-
mination.

Or was it menace?

A warning?

Whatever it was, it worked, for Stewart stared at him for
a moment, then swung on his heel and stalked back to his
car, jamming it into reverse and flying backwards before
revving the engine then driving, far too fast, out of the
hospital grounds.

As the vehicle turned, Sarah caught a glimpse of Alana
in the passenger seat and wondered what she'd made of it
all.

'I don't suppose you feel like going after him and book-
ing him for dangerous driving,' Tony said to Ken.

'What I'd really like is leave of absence, starting right
now. I don't suppose you could swing it?'

Tony grinned at him.

'I'm not nearly as powerful as any of you seem to think.
But Stewart won't let it go at that. Any minute now I could
get a call from the Minister to tell me to cease and desist.
Let's get those prints done.'

He looked at Sarah.

'You'd better come with us. Together we might hold more weight when the axe falls. Is there someone at the hospital who could sit with Lucy?'

'Sit with Lucy?' Sarah felt fear jolt her heart.

'In case he returns and starts harassing her. I don't think she should have to put up with that right now.'

The explanation sounded plausible, but it didn't entirely diminish Sarah's concern. Surely Tony couldn't think Lucy had anything to do with James's death.

'I'll send my constable over,' Ken suggested. 'It will get him out of the way at the same time. We can tell him the lass is distressed and the doctor doesn't want her left alone.'

Tony approved of this plan and the two policeman took off in the official car, leaving Sarah to check on Lucy and then follow in her own vehicle.

Lucy was sleeping, her hands tucked under her head, her pale face streaked with the grubby marks of disregarded tears. Sarah wrote a note, explaining where she'd be and that the constable was there in case she needed anything. She propped it where Lucy would see it if she woke, then, when the young man, who introduced himself as Ryan Bourke, arrived, she left the house, pleased to have another job to do.

Anything to stop her thinking about James—and Lucy— for a little longer.

'We'll do the prints, and you record them,' Tony suggested when she arrived at the small station.

Was he as keen to keep her busy as she was to have some occupation? she wondered.

She'd seen the process before, the careful blowing of the dust across the surface of the object, then the delicate task of lifting the prints onto a piece of tape before pressing them onto an evidence card. But the procedure still fascinated her so Tony had to remind her she was supposed to be doing the recording, not taking lessons.

Card 1 held the prints from the glass numbered '1' on

her sketch, card 2 took the prints from the first of the coffee-mugs, found beneath the sun-lounge where James had,
according to the guests, been lying when everyone had re-
tired for the night.

They worked their way through the seven such ordinary-
looking objects, returning the cups and glasses to the paper
evidence bags when the job was done.

'I'll do prints from your slides now,' Ken said, 'then
we're finished. Can't do much else but write up our reports
and wait till we hear back from the city on the tests.'

He pulled the slides carefully out of the bag, touching
only the hard edges of the glass.

The prints lifted cleanly, and transferred to the cards
without a blemish.

'Fat lot of good that's done us!' Tony muttered, when
he spread the collection of cards out on the work bench.

'What do you mean?' Ken asked, and Sarah joined the
two men at the bench and peered at the cards. They told
her nothing.

'Look at the other cards,' Tony suggested. Ken looked
and obviously saw what was to be seen for he nodded at
Tony, but, as Sarah glanced along the collection, nothing
leapt out at her.

'Look!' Tony waved his hands over the first set of cards.
'You don't need to be a fingerprint expert to see the lad
didn't drink out of anything we collected.'

She wasn't an expert but she could see what he meant.
The prints were all distinctly different but the person who'd
held number 4, a glass, had also held number 6, another
glass, while one of the coffee-mugs looked as if it had
passed through three or four sets of hands. But nowhere
was there a print with the characteristic loop she could see
on James's thumbprint, or with the slight line of a scar she
had noticed on his forefinger.

'But, according to Lucy, James definitely had a cup of
coffee,' she protested. 'They argued over it.'

'Maybe he had it earlier,' Tony suggested. 'Then the cups were cleared away and the ones we've collected were from a very late night or early morning supper.'

He put an arm around her shoulders as if to say he was sorry the lead was a dead end. The weight of his arm was both novel and familiar but right now she couldn't be distracted by comforting arms. Since Stewart McMurray had dragged Lucy into things, Sarah's motherly instincts were on full alert, and finding out what had happened to James had become a doubly urgent priority.

'But if his cup wasn't there, then surely knowing who *was* drinking from them later becomes even more important,' Sarah said slowly. 'One of those people should be able to tell us whether James was by the pool late in the evening, and, if he was, whether he was sleeping, drinking or fooling around enough to have been likely to slip.'

Ken shook his head.

'Some of the house guests were a little blurry about details when I questioned them this morning. but no one's admitted being out by the pool after midnight. I'll get my notes.'

He walked away. Somewhere a phone rang, and was quickly silenced. Tony poked his head into the inner office, said something to Ken, then turned back to Sarah.

'He's caught up with another matter. I told him I'd catch up with him later. Have a look at his notes then,' he said, and motioned her towards the front door.

Sarah moved obediently, but her mind was still on the previous evening's scenario.

'What time did you leave?' she asked, pausing in the doorway.

'An hour or so after you. We plebs are staying at the motel, although Ned's a guest at Craigmoor. I believe they had half a dozen house guests, mostly people honouring the festivities with a visit.'

'Which makes it seem more likely to be an accident,'

Sarah murmured, diverted by this small detail which didn't seem quite right. 'I mean, who'd murder someone with the Minister for Police in residence at the house?'

Tony nodded, but didn't seem convinced. He rubbed his hand across his face and Sarah saw tiredness had scored the new lines more deeply.

'And did you all kick on after the party?' she asked. 'Make a night of it?'

He smiled at her.

'I have no idea what the others did, but I went to bed quite early. Though not to sleep. Every time I closed my eyes I saw this gorgeous golden woman in a skimpy black dress, legs going on for ever, green-gold eyes wide with wonder and pink lips opening to my kiss.'

His husky whisper seemed to trail down Sarah's spine.

She should say something, anything, to bring things back to normal, but words were beyond her, and normality was so far away she doubted she'd ever regain it.

'No doubt you slept as soundly as ever, with no ghosts disturbing your slumber,' he added, humour glinting in his eyes.

She felt heat she thought she'd lost years ago rise to her cheeks, and stumbled into an excuse.

'I'd had a difficult delivery and practically no sleep the night before,' she told him, and he chuckled at her defence.

'Hey, I believe you,' he said, raising his hands in a gesture of surrender. 'I know how important it is for a doctor to cultivate an ability to sleep whenever and wherever possible. Policemen should learn from them.'

There was a pause, then he flicked her lightly on the chin.

'I'm glad to find you can still do it, although I'm egotistical enough to have hoped I might have disturbed your dreams.'

Not my dreams, but every waking moment, Sarah thought, but she held her tongue. Tony was here for three days, and although the death of someone they'd both loved had drawn them together, there was too much old baggage between them for things to develop in so short a time.

'Not biting? Well, I can't say I blame you. Can you give me a lift back to the hospital? I left my car there.'

She blinked away an image of 'things developing'—a pleasant and exciting image—and tried to work out what he'd asked.

Car. Hospital.

'Of course.' She looked into his face and saw concern and affection there.

Love?

She shivered.

'Did you get a cup of coffee when you took Lucy home?' he asked. 'Something to eat?'

He didn't wait for her to think back, but seized her elbow and hustled her towards her car, opening the passenger door and practically dumping her inside.

'Keys?' he demanded, sliding in behind the wheel. 'Oh, they're in here. That's another bad habit you've retained.'

'Another?' she asked weakly, bemused by this masterful behaviour.

He didn't answer immediately, starting the car and doing a U-turn outside the station.

'Going without food, not looking after yourself properly.' He grinned at her but kept on scolding. 'You know you're no good in the morning without your caffeine fix and some food in your stomach, yet you keep going and going until you're ready to pass out.'

He pulled up further down the main street, outside the old Acropolis Café.

'Come on. There's someone watching Lucy. Let's get you some late breakfast. Or should that be an early lunch?'

She was about to protest when her stomach, perhaps awoken to its emptiness by his words, growled loudly.

'Don't you dare say I told you so,' she warned Tony,

then she clambered out of the car because the warmth in his eyes had nothing to do with breakfast but with a hunger of another kind.

A hunger she recognised in her own body but didn't want to consider right now.

'Town's quiet,' Tony remarked, as he joined her on the footpath.

'There's a ''Breakfast in the Park'' do on this morning, followed by the school fête,' she told him. 'In fact, you should probably be at one or other venue, squiring your Minister around.'

'He can't get into too much trouble at breakfast, surely. Or at the school fête,' Tony replied, walking into the café beside her and looking around as if to check if anything had changed. 'Besides, he's sent me on a mission. He won't expect me to be there.'

'He probably doesn't expect you to be here either,' Sarah pointed out, greeting old George Constantine with a wave.

'Ah, Tony! You came back to get your lady. I am pleased to see this.' Old George bustled forward to welcome them both, Sarah with a kiss and Tony with a warm handclasp. 'You need breakfast? I hear about what's happened. A dreadful thing for that young man to die.'

He bustled away, muttering about coffee, and Sarah, who'd been eating in the café on and off all week because she'd had little time for cooking, slid into a seat and put James's death firmly from her mind. Later, she'd grieve for him. Right now she needed food and answers.

Or questions that might lead to answers.

'So, you will eat an omelette? Scrambled eggs? Tony, a full breakfast?' George had returned and was pouring two coffees. Then he folded his hands expectantly over his full belly while he waited for their order.

'A small omelette,' Sarah told him, and, when Tony had suggested he make it two, the old man walked away.

'He's got to be a hundred,' Tony whispered to her.

'Eighty-five,' Sarah replied. 'I asked him.'

'Does he still run the place on his own?'

Sarah nodded.

'He gets someone in to clean each evening, and a young woman who's new to town makes the cakes and serves at the counter during the busy time of the day, but apart from that it's just George.'

'But wasn't his son a doctor? And another one became a lawyer, if I remember rightly. Why's he still working here, not living in comfortable retirement by the beach somewhere?'

'The shop's his life and he loves it,' Sarah reminded him. 'He's got grandsons and granddaughters who are doctors now. He's so proud of his family, but this—the café, the town—is where he feels he belongs.'

Tony met her eyes across the table.

'Do you feel like that about your place at the beach? About any place?'

She started to say yes, then realised it wasn't entirely true. She loved the beach house, and always felt relaxed there—but belonging?

'When Lucy and I first came to Windrush I felt I belonged,' she admitted, speaking slowly because she was facing something she hadn't considered until this very minute.

'Because of the town, or because we fell in love?'

His eyes scanned her face, as pitiless as the bright lights in an operating theatre, seeking truth.

She sipped her coffee to delay, but couldn't avoid answering.

'I've never thought about it,' she told him, 'but, yes, perhaps belonging is to do with people as well as places. George and his wife brought up their family here. His memories are all around him.'

'I didn't have an affair with Anna McMurray.'

The statement was so blunt it struck her like a physical blow, but its impact was even stronger internally.

'You could have said that eleven years ago,' she told him, hiding the joy and uncertainty seething within her.

Not that it should have mattered now.

Although it did.

'I was too proud,' he told her, taking her hand and rubbing his thumb along her fingers. 'Too stubborn. It shattered me that you could ask. That you lacked the trust I believed was an essential ingredient of love.' He lifted her hand and dropped a kiss on the palm, then folded her fingers over it and gave it back to her. 'Stupid young fool that I was!' he added harshly.

She took in the words and nodded, then rested her hand on his.

'I can remember being scared by the force of the love we felt for each other, terrified it wouldn't last. It was faith I should have had, Tony, not trust. When it all blew up I simply accepted that I wasn't meant to have that kind of joy. It was as if I'd been expecting something bad to happen. As if I'd been tempting fate by being so happy.'

'You'd had one devastating loss, with David,' Tony said softly. 'It was understandable you'd feel that way.'

She looked into his face, and shook her head.

'No, don't make excuses for me. You were right the first time. I should have believed in you, fought for your love, not let you walk away from me like that.'

'And now?'

She shrugged. 'The timing's not crash hot, is it?'

He smiled at her despair.

'We'll sort it out,' he assured her. 'You'll feel much better once you've eaten. Sarah Gilmour, Superdoctor, ready to take on the world again.'

'Superdoctor!' She whispered the word as she looked into his eyes and saw beyond the tender laughter. 'You used to call me that to tease me. When you claimed I was working too hard.'

He reached out and ran his hand across her hair, his touch soft but not seductive.

'You were, and no doubt still are, a super doctor. Which, though you may not believe it, made it seem almost right to walk away from you. Deep down, I'd always been concerned about the difference in our... I suppose status is the word. Social standing. Earning power. All those things.'

'You make it sound as if you felt inferior to me!' Sarah said uncertainly, unable to accept that such a major issue could have hovered like a dark shadow in his mind when she'd been so blissfully lost in love.

He shrugged and the lines in his face deepened as he smiled.

'We'd never talked about much the future—not in a planning sense. About what would happen if I was transferred. About your job...my job...'

'We didn't talk about much at all,' she reminded him, as she struggled to understand the reservations he'd had about their relationship. 'Our time together was too precious, as I remember. As far as I was concerned, the future would work itself out.'

He nodded to acknowledge her words, then continued what he'd been saying. 'Anyway, when it all blew up in my face, I let my anger tell me that what we had would never have lasted. That you'd eventually have wanted someone better.'

'Better?' Sarah echoed as surprise warred with disbelief.

Tony looked at her for a moment, then leaned forward as if about to say something important. But George appeared, and all he said was, 'Ah! Breakfast.'

They sat back to allow George access to the table, and the sight of the golden omelette and the pile of fresh, crisp toast brought Sarah from the past to the present in an instant.

She was on her second piece of toast when a teenager ran into the café.

'Someone said you were here, Doctor. Could you come? An urn tipped over at the hamburger stand at the school fête. The ambulance is there but Eddie asked me to find you so you could meet them at the hospital.'

'Them?' Sarah muttered as she stood up and brushed crumbs from her jeans, then stepped out from the booth.

'A lady who was serving, and two kids who were playing near the table. The kids probably knocked the trestle holding it up,' the youth explained as she accompanied him to the door.

Which was where she remembered Tony.

And Lucy.

She turned back to where he was explaining the emergency to George.

'You go,' Tony said, throwing the car keys to her. 'I'll walk back to the cottage and keep an eye on Lucy.'

The rush of warmth she felt had nothing to do with physical attraction this time. It was more to do with security.

With belonging.

CHAPTER FIVE

FORGET belonging and think about burns. Scalds. Stabilise the patient first, then check the degree of involvement and the percentage of body surface area affected.

By the time Sarah arrived at the hospital her mind was back in work mode—which was just as well as one child was screaming lustily while his mother was swearing equally loudly—and threatening to sue the school board for negligence.

Another woman was sitting on a chair against the wall, a towel wrapped around her waist and a look of stoic endurance on her sun-lined face.

Eddie waved to her and indicated he'd put a patient in the enclosed trauma unit. That would be the first priority.

Emmie arrived, no doubt alerted by the noise.

'Could you assess the screamer?' Sarah asked her. 'First-degree burns are usually the most painful so it's my guess that's his problem. Immerse the burned area in water to cool it. Call me if you need me.'

She paused to speak to the woman, who lifted the towel to show angry red streaks on her stomach, moist blisters already rising.

'See to the other child,' the woman said. 'I can wait.'

At that moment a second nurse arrived, so Sarah explained what she wanted done and headed for the trauma unit.

The young woman who stood beside the gurney, anxiously smoothing her child's hair back from his forehead, looked familiar.

'I'm Carey Winter. You delivered my first baby, Brooke. She was supposed to be watching this little larrikin, but I can't blame her—he's like greased lightning. Aren't you, Charlie?'

She was making an effort to sound relaxed but her voice was tight with anxiety.

'No-one can keep them safe all the time,' Sarah told her, thinking of James, of Lucy's pain. The child was lying on his left side, a sterile sheet covering his body. Eddie had started a drip and colourless fluid was flowing slowly into his arm.

'Hello, Charlie,' she said gently, and her heart clenched as the little fellow smiled.

Lifting the sheet, she realised that the full force of the water must have cascaded down his back, hottest where it hit his neck. She bent closer and was relieved to see it was on the posterior surface only—no circumferential burning. Moving quickly now, she skimmed through Eddie's findings, the analgesia already administered, checked the flow on the drip, then dumped the file on the bench and slipped on a sterile gown.

She scrubbed her hands and dried them, pulled on gloves, tied a mask around her neck, then said apologetically, 'All this gear makes things look worse than they are. It's a precaution against infecting the wound. Let's take a closer look.'

The nurse she'd left with the injured woman materialised.

'Sister sent me in. She said she can manage out there.'

Sarah nodded to her then turned her attention back to the little boy who was watching her with wide brown eyes.

'I'm going to see what I can do to make you feel a bit better. Is it hurting?'

He nodded gravely but, knowing the wound was secondary to his physical condition, she took the child's blood pressure and pulse while the nurse donned her sterile garb.

'When someone gets burned, we try to work out how much of the body is affected,' she told the little boy, although the information was more for his mother than for him. 'You were lucky the hot water missed your head and only got your back. Backs are better places for burns than heads. How old are you, Charlie?'

'Five.'

The answer pleased her. Although his pulse was slightly higher than normal for a child, it wasn't racing and his blood pressure was good. Confusion was another pointer to circulatory problems, but if he knew his age...

'And did you have a tetanus injection before you started school?'

'Don't go to school yet,' he told her.

'He's up to date with all his shots,' Carey assured her.

'School next year?' Sarah asked him, nodding to the nurse who was holding up a scalpel blade and scalpel.

She straightened up and turned to Carey.

'The burns are not good but not that bad. Most of them would be classified as second degree but within the more moderate range. They cover what we'd consider to be about twelve per cent of his body, which is enough for concern but not for panic. I can keep him here, take the tops off the larger blisters and put a dry dressing over them and antibacterial cream over the others. We need to change the dressings twice a day and watch closely to make sure the wounds don't become infected.'

She paused, knowing Carey needed time to assimilate what she was saying.

'Or I can send him to town where they'll do much the same thing, only if he's there the flying surgeon could take a look at him next Tuesday.'

'The flying surgeon? You think he might need a skin graft?' Carey asked. 'Is that why the surgeon would have a look?'

Sarah nodded.

'What do you think?' Carey asked her.

'He's young and healthy. I think the skin will heal well.

He's a boy and, although I don't like to sound sexist, even mild scars that a girl would hate as she grew older could be considered a real macho thing for a boy.'

Carey smiled.

'Do I have to decide right now? My husband's dropping the other kids at his mother's place. He'll be here soon.'

Sarah touched her lightly on the shoulder.

'There's no hurry,' she assured her. 'I'll tackle the blisters and dress them. I'd do that anyway, whether he's staying with us or going to Karunga.'

She scrubbed again and put on clean gloves before she began, talking all the time to the little boy about games he liked to play and the songs he sang at kindergarten.

The drug Eddie had administered in the drip was dulling Charlie's pain and easing his anxiety, but Sarah could feel Carey's tension as she stood beside her son, holding his free hand.

Emmie came in as Sarah finished and produced dressings and silver sulphadiazine cream.

'Well, Charlie Winter. You've really done it this time, haven't you?' she said to their patient.

'He's only been home a month,' Carey explained to Sarah. 'Broken leg last time. Emmie's always teasing him about liking hospital better than his home.'

'Some kids are just born accident-prone,' Emmie told her placidly. 'Isn't Charlie the one who arrived in the middle of the bushfire scare?'

'My mum had me in the fire engine,' Charlie piped up, and although his voice was sleepy Sarah was again relieved that he was able to follow what was being said—and add to it! It gave her confidence in her decision to offer to care for him here, if the parents happened to choose that option.

'The other child?' Sarah asked Emmie, as they finished tending the wounds and moved away from the table.

'He's fine. First degree, very superficial. The water splashed his arms and touched the side of his face, but my guess is he was far enough away for it to have been cooler by the time it hit him.'

A tall, dark-tanned man came in and Carey fell into his arms. Sarah felt a jolt of jealousy as the man comforted his wife, then held her clamped to his side as he bent to look at his little boy.

'Charlie, Charlie, Charlie,' he said gruffly, smiling in spite of the huskiness in his voice.

'Dad, Dad, Dad,' the youngster replied, in what was obviously a well-rehearsed routine.

The father ruffled his hair and whispered, 'You'll be right, mate.' Then he straightened up to look at Sarah. 'He will be right?' he asked, and Carey answered first.

'Let's go outside. I'll tell you there.' She bent and kissed Charlie's cheek. 'We'll only be a minute and Emmie will stay with you,' she promised him, then she tugged her husband's arm and together they left the room.

'I bet you offered to keep him here,' Emmie said to Sarah.

'You know I hate sending kids away. It's so disruptive for the family.'

'I know! I actually agree, but he'll need careful handling.'

'Sterile, not careful,' Sarah reminded her. 'And twice a day. Have you the staff to handle it?'

'I guess so,' Emmie agreed, 'but Charlie's a one to one. Turn your back and he's likely to be operating on someone before you know where you are.'

'Can his family help?' Sarah asked, knowing Emmie understood the dynamics of most of the families in town.

'To a point. There are three other kids, but they're all at school so Carey can spend most days here. Ewan's mother's great. She'll come in whenever she can.'

'So we should be able to manage him?'

'Sure thing. Especially with the place as quiet as it is. Speaking of managing...?' Emmie said softly, and Sarah knew the conversation had changed, although her friend wouldn't ask direct questions about James's death in front of a patient—however small he was.

'I'm OK.'

'And Lucy?' Emmie persisted.

Sarah lifted her shoulders in an I-don't-know gesture.

'She was sleeping. Tony's there.'

'She'll take it hard,' Emmie said, then she blinked away a few tears. 'But won't we all? He was a great kid and he turned into a fine young man.'

She looked anxiously at Sarah.

'He never struck me as being depressed...'

'Me neither,' Sarah told her, but she wondered why Emmie would have said that. Unless rumours of suicide were already spreading along the town's grapevine. 'In fact, I know he wasn't.'

She didn't actually *know*, because it wasn't possible to know how someone else was feeling deep inside, but she was going to scotch the rumours this time—not listen to them.

She'd show her faith and trust—although in James this time, not Tony.

'I don't for a minute think he killed himself,' she added firmly.

Carey and Ewan returned and faced her.

'We'd rather he stayed here,' they said in unison. 'We know he's a nuisance for the staff, so we'll try to have someone with him all the time.'

She glanced to where her child was sleeping.

'Well, once he's feeling better he'll be a nuisance,' she added softly.

'We'll take him through to the ward and settle him into a bed,' Emmie told them, signalling to the nurse to call an orderly. 'Why don't you stay in case he wakes when we transfer him, then shoot off for a while? It might be your last few hours together for a few days.'

'We should go back to the fête,' Carey said, obviously anxious about doing the right thing for everyone.

'Mum's taking the other kids back there so that lets us out,' her husband told her. 'Once we've seen him settled, we'll leave him with the nurses and grab a cup of coffee. As Emmie says, it's going to be a long week.'

Sarah saw the love in his eyes as he looked at his wife, and again felt envy surge through her.

'Not all marriages are made in heaven,' Emmie reminded her dryly as the nurse and orderly wheeled the gurney out of the room. 'I'd best go with them. You take care of yourself, and give Lucy a big hug for me.'

Sarah watched her friend depart. Hugging her daughter seemed like a good idea but first she'd better do a quick ward round, see how Bessie was this morning. And Shelley and the baby.

It was early afternoon by the time she'd finished at the hospital, and she was glad she'd had time to eat half the omelette before being called in. Leg-weary and emotionally drained, she trudged across to the cottage to find a tousle-haired Lucy at the dining table, her head bent over a steaming cup of coffee.

'That smells like salvation,' Sarah said to the tall, familiar, yet unfamiliar figure hovering in the kitchen. 'And if there's food that goes with it, count me in.'

'How can you eat?' Lucy demanded, looking up from the coffee for long enough to scowl at her mother.

'Early training,' Sarah told her cheerfully, refusing to acknowledge either the scowl or her daughter's tone of voice. 'A doctor soon learns to eat whenever food is offered—that way you don't faint onto the patient's body cavity in the middle of emergency surgery.'

The fair head lifted again, the scowl more mutinous than ever.

'You know I don't mean that!' Lucy muttered, and Sarah

stepped towards her and wrapped her arms around her shoulders.

'I know you didn't, love. And feel free to be as horrid as you like. Whatever helps you is OK with me. I eat because not eating isn't going to bring James back, and because my body needs food, particularly if I want my brain to work.'

'He didn't kill himself,' Lucy told her, then she pushed the coffee away and folded her arms on the table, before dropping her head to rest on them.

'I know he didn't, Lucy,' Sarah whispered, patting the shaking shoulders.

'But can you prove it?' her daughter cried. 'Or will everyone have to believe whatever she tells them?'

'She?'

'Alana!'

The word was muffled but still distinguishable.

'Why would she spread stories?'

Lucy raised her head again and said spitefully, 'Because she's like that.'

Sarah closed her eyes, but Tony saved her from answering.

'Not good enough, Lucy,' he said firmly. 'Give us something definite, something we can go on.'

Lucy turned her glare on him, then swiped away her tears before answering. 'She's protecting Stewart. Diverting attention away from him. Getting people talking so no one looks too closely into other things that went on.' She paused, then added almost under her breath, 'James had a fight with his father.'

'That's not new,' Tony pointed out. 'He was always fighting with his father.'

Lucy slumped back in the chair now, her arms crossed across her chest—defensive in the face of Tony's remark.

He leaned forward across the kitchen divider and Sarah

said goodbye to thoughts of coffee. This was Tony the policeman now, and her instinct was to protect her daughter.

'Did you hear the fight?' Tony asked.

Lucy nodded.

'How late was this?'

'About eleven—maybe later. Most of the guests had gone, and the house guests were on the front verandah. There was a moon and they were going gaga over it and how clear the stars were in the country.'

'And where was James?'

'He was on a lounger by the pool. He had a cup of coffee. I told Mum about it, about him saying it was more a symbol than coffee. I got huffy with him and went inside. That's when I heard the argument.'

'Heard both voices? James's and Stewart's?'

'James's definitely, and a deep voice. It sounded like Stewart and he was talking about Craigmoor, on and on about James not wanting to run the property, so I assumed it was Stewart.'

'Most likely it was,' Tony said, then, as suddenly as the questioning had begun, it stopped, for he turned to Sarah and said, 'Coffee coming right up. What do you want on a sandwich? I've already checked your meagre supplies of food. You've a choice of cheese or strawberry jam.'

'Mum will have both. She's a cheese and jam freak,' Lucy told him, and Sarah realised that forcing her daughter to talk had helped.

She looked across at the man she'd loved so desperately and nodded acknowledgment. He was a nice man as well as a good cop.

'Did you see James again later?' Tony asked as he worked at the kitchen bench.

'No!'

The single word held such pathos that Sarah dropped into a chair beside Lucy and took her hand as her daughter explained.

'But I know he came into the bedroom later. I heard him and woke up then stupidly went back to sleep.'

'You know someone came into the room,' Sarah reminded her. 'You don't know that it was James.'

'I guess not,' Lucy said, then her brow wrinkled as she said, 'But who else would it have been? It had to have been James.'

Tony arrived with the sandwich and coffee. He set both in front of Sarah, then pressed her shoulder as if to warn her not to say any more.

Did he want Lucy puzzling over it for some reason?

Sarah drank some coffee and bit into the sandwich while Tony went back to retrieve his own coffee, before joining them at the table.

'I want you to think back, Lucy,' he said calmly. 'Someone came into the room, and something woke you. Can you remember what?'

Lucy's eyes, greener than Sarah's own, grew wide, then she frowned as she tried to relive that moment.

'Damn!' she muttered, shaking her head and sending her blonde hair flying. 'It must have been a noise of some kind that woke me, but it wasn't distinct enough to remember. Perhaps the doorhandle turning.'

'That's OK, stay with the memory,' Tony said easily. 'Now, what did the person do?'

'Went to the lowboy. I remember that because I thought it was James and imagined he was taking things out of his pocket. He does that even if we go to the beach for a swim. Takes everything out of his pockets and sets them in a little pile on his handkerchief.'

Sarah glanced at Tony, wanting to tell him James's pockets hadn't been emptied. He caught her eye and gave an almost imperceptible shake of his head. She stayed silent.

'Then what?' he prompted Lucy.

Tears welled up again, and Sarah felt the slim fingers tighten on hers.

'I must have gone back to sleep. I can't remember anything until I woke in the morning—this morning.'

She shuddered convulsively. Sarah let her cry, and when the worst of it was over she walked Lucy back into the bedroom, murmuring all the platitudes that were paraded for use in cases of sudden death but were all humans had available by way of verbal comfort.

'I'll be OK, Mum. I'm just so tired,' Lucy told her, snuggling under the blanket and once again curling into a tight ball.

'Nature provides its own sedation,' Sarah told Tony as she walked wearily back to the table.

'But not for you?' he said gently, then he stepped behind her and began to massage her neck and shoulders.

'That is so wonderful,' she said, moving beneath the ministrations of his hands.

'I have my uses,' he said modestly. 'And when I'm done here, I'll heat up your coffee and insist you eat that sandwich. Cheese and jam!' He shuddered. 'No one else would want it.'

The tension was easing out of her body, and she slumped back in the chair and looked up to thank him.

She caught the dark sheen in his eyes, and held her breath.

'It's been a long time, Sarah,' he murmured.

She nodded, but when he bent towards her she moved so their lips would meet, so she could kiss him as well as he kiss her.

'My love!'

The words were a prayer wrenched from deep within him, brushed across her lips like an added blessing.

They moved apart, but only so she could stand up and fit her body to his shape, nestle against him and kiss him properly. This time it was she who spoke, his name a mere whisper of delight as the years of wanting him melted away, and even the sorrow of James's death was somehow eased by the magic of being in Tony's arms again.

'Did you, or Ken, check out James's room?'

The thought occurred so forcibly, arrowing through the haze of sexual contentment and delight, that she broke away from him and asked it as it struck.

He looked down into her face, his eyes still dark with passion, his lips blurred by kisses, his smile wry.

'To quote your daughter, "Sheesh!" Where did that come from? Have you been thinking murder the entire time I've been kissing you?'

She felt her cheeks heat with far-too-youthful embarrassment and shook her head.

'I was as surprised by it as you were but, now it's out, did you?'

His brow puckered in a frown and she lifted her hand to smooth the crease away. She felt safe and secure with his arms around her—his body her rock in this particular storm.

'I went in there with Ken. It was fairly bare. No youthful souvenirs, soccer medals, much-loved toys. More a visitor's room than a testimony to his childhood.'

'A visitor's room. Well, that probably *was* a testimony to his childhood!' Sarah told him. 'After all, once his mother had died and he was sent away to boarding school, that's all he was at Craigmoor. A visitor.'

The sadness she felt now was for the child James.

'You gave him happiness in his holidays with you and Lucy,' Tony told her, folding her back into his arms, but this time for comfort not passion. 'Gave him the family he missed out on at Craigmoor.'

'I hope so,' she said, and snuggled closer, then, just as her body was again seduced by his, she remembered the question.

'He had stuff in his pockets,' she said, pushing far enough away from him to look up into his face. 'A handkerchief, pen, a notebook. Don't you see? If it wasn't James unloading his pockets which Lucy heard, someone else came in. To take something perhaps.'

Tony brushed his lips across her nose but she realised he barely knew he was doing it. He was focussed on some internal considerations.

'Ken listed what he found. There was a small overnight bag, open, but with the clothes still in it—James hadn't unpacked anything into drawers or the wardrobe. On the lowboy, there was a hairbrush and a toiletries bag—a big, green mannish affair with toothbrush, toothpaste, razor, shaving cream, tablets, deodorant, aftershave lotion.'

'Tablets? What tablets?'

Tony seemed startled by her abrupt demand. He puzzled over it, as if scanning his memory for a clue.

'I didn't look and Ken didn't say. I remember they were in a small white bottle, not in a plastic and foil blister pack.'

Sarah moved out of the protective arms, needing to pace as she considered this.

'Lucy hasn't mentioned him being sick. Perhaps they were vitamins.'

'No. They were definitely prescription drugs of some kind—they had his name on them.'

'Well, they must be his—have been his. I wonder…'

'We don't have to wonder. I'll phone Ken. He's very thorough in spite of his reluctance. He'll have written it all down—just as a precaution. You really scared him by insisting he take all the cups and glasses from around the pool.'

Sarah stopped her pacing to turn back towards him as doubt bit into her again.

'And you? Did it scare you?'

He smiled and moved towards her, taking her in his arms before saying gently, 'My first thought was pride—that I'd taught you so well, way back when you first visited an accident scene.' He punctuated the sentence with a kiss. 'My second was that I was glad you'd done it. I won't allow myself to be manipulated this time, Sarah. I promise you that.'

Another kiss, but she sensed he hadn't finished speaking. Hoped he hadn't, if he kept up the punctuation.

'But at present it might work more in our favour if I'm seen to be on the side of might and power. I will help you all I can, and bolster Ken if he falters in his duty, but as long as the Minister thinks I'm working to make things right for the McMurrays I've a chance of staying on until all this is sorted out.'

No kiss that time. Only a sense of trepidation.

'And if not? If you're yanked away, or kept by your master's side and have to leave on Monday? What then?'

He looked into her eyes, his face intent—almost grave.

'I'll resign. I've done my time and could probably get a civilian job that would use my administrative skills if nothing else. Perhaps even a consultancy in big business.'

'You'd resign to stay here and find out what happened to James?'

Sarah hid the leap of hope this thought had generated.

'No,' he said gently, kissing her for the comma this time. 'I'd resign to stay here, to be close to you. To serve you and support you in any way I can. To prove to you that what I feel for you goes way beyond the physical and to convince you that we've already wasted far too much time, being apart.'

Sarah felt her own love unfurling deep inside her, warming her body, calming her mind. One tiny voice of caution whispered warnings, but if she wanted him so badly, needed him to make her life complete, could it be wrong?

She leaned into the kiss, and let the magic of their physical attraction take over, bringing her long-dormant feelings and desires back to surging, aching life.

Until another problem twanged in her brain—slow-motion thinking!

She pushed away again. 'Was the tablet bottle full?'

Again dazed eyes looked into hers, and this time the grin was more rueful than wry.

'Perhaps we should cease all intimacy until this problem is solved. I hate to think what it could do to my manhood if you suddenly had an idea in the middle of a hot sexual encounter.'

'I'm sorry,' she said. 'It's not as if I'm not enjoying the kissing. It's just that these ideas keep popping into my head. It's because I'm upset about James, and worried about Lucy. She needs to know what happened in order to accept his death.'

She paused then matched his rueful grin with one of her own. 'I need to know, too. I loved him, Tony. As if he were my own.'

He held her for a long moment.

'I know that,' he said. 'What if I phone Ken and find out about the tablets? If you know what they are, you'll work out why he needed them. It will be another loose end tied off.'

He led her back to the table where cold coffee and a dry sandwich still awaited her.

'I'll toast that for you in a minute,' he said, whipping both the sandwich and the coffee-cup away.

Sarah smiled, thinking how nice it was to have someone looking after her. Someone to care whether she ate or not! She watched him fussing in the kitchen, putting on the kettle, dialling the police station, tucking the phone under his ear as he melted a little pat of butter in a frying pan to toast her sandwich.

But when he spoke to someone then shook his head, she knew the plan had been frustrated.

'He's on his way to town with the specimens and, as far as the constable can see, hasn't typed up any of his notes as yet.'

'Well, he wouldn't have. He's been busy both at Craigmoor and in town, I imagine,' Sarah replied, then she sighed with pleasurable hunger as the toasted sandwich and fresh coffee were put in front of her.

'He must be contactable in his car,' Tony said, sitting down opposite her and urging her, with a hand gesture, to eat.

'He'd be in radio contact with the station,' Sarah agreed. 'Is it so urgent?'

Tony shrugged.

'I guess not, although it's niggling at me now. When I close my eyes I can see the lowboy. There was nothing else on it. Nothing in the drawers, yet Lucy's impression was that someone was there for some time. She might not have said that in so many words, but for her to think James was emptying his pockets there has to be an element of time. Watch.'

He stood up and moved to the divider between the kitchen and the living-dining room, then reached into his hip pocket and removed his wallet. He set it on the bench. Removed a handkerchief from the right hand front pocket, then dug his fingers into his fob pocket.

Brought them out empty.

'He might not have been carrying change so we'll leave that.'

Now he took a pen and slim notebook from his shirt pocket, then turned towards her.

'See, it takes time—thirty seconds or so. We men are creatures of habit. We like to have these odds and ends about our person. If it wasn't James who came in, what did the other person do?'

'Feel around in the dark? Perhaps looking for something? Did he or she come in to take something?' Sarah guessed.

'Or leave something,' Tony countered, and she felt a chill where so much warmth had been.

CHAPTER SIX

'THE tablets? No, that can't be right. Not if the tablets were in James's name.' Sarah stumbled to a halt.

'I think we should confirm that. I'll go out there and check, perhaps bag and label everything in the room.'

'That's keeping very low key, Officer Kemp, as far as the McMurrays are concerned,' Sarah pointed out.

'You're right, and it probably exceeds my authority in the case. Damn. I'll have to send the constable and somehow make him think the order came from Griffiths so he doesn't have to lie.'

'Radio Ken and ask him to send his henchman. There's a radio in Cas for the ambulance. Come on.'

They crossed to the hospital—a mistake in itself, Sarah realised, when she saw the number of people sitting wanly in the waiting room.

'I'll be with you in a minute,' she promised the harassed nurse who was trying to keep order.

She led Tony to the small office and showed him the card with the call signs, then went out to ask what was happening.

'It's the school fête,' the nurse who'd been on duty earlier told her. 'Something's being sold there that's reacting within an hour on people's stomachs. Cramping pains and nausea. Some vomiting.'

Sarah looked around the room and imagined it twice as full if they didn't stop the consumption of the mystery product.

'Attention, everyone,' she called out, and got a slight lessening of the noise.

'Put up your hands if you've been to the school fête.'

A forest of hands shot into the air.

'And who had something to eat there?'

One hundred per cent reply again.

'OK, it's something you bought there, so let's go quickly around the room and each person tell me exactly what you ate.'

By the time the eighth person had mentioned hamburgers, Sarah had her culprit.

'I could try to phone the school, but as I'll need samples to send away for testing I might just as well go down there.' She turned to the nurse. 'Can you manage here?'

The nurse nodded. 'I'm dividing them into order according to how sick they are, and Emmie's checking their history and doling out antiemetics and electrolyte replacement sachets.'

'Thank heaven for Emmie,' Sarah muttered, and hurried away, anxious to stop hamburger sales before things got worse.

Tony caught up with her as she reached the door and took her by the elbow.

'Come on,' he said. 'There's been an accident. Ken Griffiths has just crashed. I heard it happen.'

'I can't! An accident? Where? It might be faster to get someone from town if he was on his way there. I've got to go over to the school. They're poisoning people.'

But she let him guide her and realised they were heading for her car, not his. It had her bag in it—was he thinking that far ahead? Seeing Ken as the priority?

'We'll stop at the station and send the constable to the school. Food poisoning?'

She nodded.

'Hamburgers,' she explained, doing up her seat belt as he started the car. Somehow it was easier to obey orders than to try to think herself.

'I'll get him to call the ambulance as well. Ken hadn't got far. He was rounding the corner at Blight's Bridge, said he heard a shot and the car went out of control. I heard a grinding, tearing noise then couldn't raise him.'

'Heard a shot?' Sarah wondered if she sounded as hysterical as she felt.

She must have for Tony patted her knee.

'It could have been a tyre bursting,' he told her as he pulled up outside the police station. 'I'll be back in a minute. It's the hamburgers you want?'

'Tell the constable to take the lot—meat, buns, salads—bag them separately and take the bags to the hospital. With a mass outbreak like this I'll have to track it down and make a full report to the Health Department. In fact, ask him to close the stall and get everyone out of it. It could be something like salmonella bacteria on the cutting boards. I should be there!'

She fretted at the delay although she knew a life was more important than finding the source of infection in her other patients, none of whom had seemed particularly ill.

'We won't be long. If you're not needed on site you can come right back,' Tony promised when he returned.

'*I* can come right back?'

He was looking straight ahead, focussed on the road as they sped out of town. She could hear the wail of the ambulance siren coming up behind them, but it couldn't blot out the fear that rode with them in the car.

The horror his words had prompted!

'Someone should see the samples get to town,' he said quietly, confirming her worst thoughts.

'Accidents do happen,' she reminded him, switching sides in an effort to allay her own suspicions.

'Of course,' he said, but the words brought little comfort, his tone of voice too bland to carry any conviction.

The big, heavy, four-wheel-drive vehicle was wrapped around a huge river gum just to the right of the bridge, and as Tony popped the boot of the car Sarah sprang out, grabbed her bag and ran towards the mangled vehicle.

Ken was wedged between an inflated airbag and the car seat, held tightly in place by his seat belt.

He was also conscious.

'I'm OK,' he told her, 'but I can't move my legs and the damn seat belt's jammed so I can't get it off. Is Tony with you?'

Sarah, who already had Ken's wrist in her hand and was counting the beats of his pulse, nodded her head.

'Tell him to stay with the car,' Ken muttered, then he passed out, slumping forward, the airbag acting like a large pillow for his head.

'I think it's pain, not blood loss,' she told Tony, who was close behind her. 'I can't feel the wetness of blood. Here. Can you cut away the airbag?'

She handed him scissors then heard the ambulance pull up. Now they'd have the equipment to release him and move him safely.

They worked as a team, Sarah starting a drip so she could give him IV pain relief, the ambulance bearers stabilising his neck and back, while Tony tried to figure out the best way to release his legs.

'He slewed sideways into the tree so I'd say his ankles and feet are trapped, rather than the upper leg.'

Sarah, who had felt down as far as Ken's knees, confirmed the thighs were free of obstruction. Whatever was holding him was further down.

Using the big mechanical jaws carried by the ambulance, the side panels were ripped and twisted open, then the winch on the front of the ambulance towed the wrecked vehicle free of the tree. By wrenching the front seat off its moorings, they were finally able to free Ken and lift him onto a stretcher.

'He'll have to go to town, and possibly be flown from there to a base hospital for orthopaedic surgery,' Sarah told Eddie.

She made a note of what she'd administered on the chart

that would travel with him and sent them on their way, after confirming they'd radioed for a tow truck.

'I've got to get back,' she told Tony. 'All hell was breaking loose when I left.'

He touched her shoulder, then kissed her cheek.

'Ken said to stay with the truck,' she muttered. 'He wasn't convinced it was blow-out, was he?'

Tony shook his head.

'You drive carefully,' he warned. 'And slowly. No more accidents today.'

She promised she would, but hated leaving him, feeling, for the first time in all her years in the bush, an alien quality about its stillness.

Approaching town, she recalled the conversation they'd been having before going across to the hospital. Now *she'd* have to see if she could talk the young constable into going out to the house and removing James's belongings.

Which she doubted he'd do on her authority!

He was at the hospital, hovering over the plastic bags of limp food, watching anxiously through the window as the last of the patients were sent home.

'I put him in the little lab,' Emmie had told Sarah when she'd walked back into Cas. 'But how you're going to handle all that stuff, I don't know. And the people running the fête will probably want your blood!'

'Better to have a little of my blood split than the entire town in hospital with food poisoning,' Sarah had said. 'Are you managing here?'

'Just about clear. You go and find the source of the problem.'

'I'd have had a hamburger if I'd been at the fête,' Ryan told Sarah as she hurried into the small laboratory between the outpatient and casualty rooms. 'How's Ken? Is he OK? Did he really have an accident? He must drive that road twice a week. Makes it hard to believe, doesn't it?'

'Accidents can happen to anyone any time,' she reminded him, sounding old and pompous in an effort to cover her own fears about the 'accident'. 'I don't suppose you thought to bring the cutting boards?'

He rummaged through his collection of plastic bags and produced one that held not only cutting boards but knives, metal tongs and barbecue tools.

'I reckoned the tools would have scrapings from the barbecue on them in case the problem was there.'

'Great work,' Sarah said, then hesitated, wondering how she could persuade him go out to Craigmoor without making it obvious it was her suggestion.

'Tony Kemp phoned you earlier about Ken's list of what was in James's bedroom out at McMurrays,' she began.

'It must still be in Ken's notebook,' Ryan told her.

'Which right now, if it's still intact, is on its way to hospital in town. I'm anxious to know if there were any drugs out there. If the lab tests find drugs, we're going to be asked questions about where they might have originated.'

Ryan's eyes lit up and Sarah knew she had him hooked.

'I could go out to Craigmoor and get his stuff,' he offered. 'It's best to have it out of the house in case someone tampers with it.'

'Great idea!' Sarah told him. 'I'm particularly interested in a bottle of tablets Tony said was in James's toilet bag when he and Ken checked the bedroom. Maybe he took a sleeping tablet on a regular basis and last night, with the party and all, decided to take an extra dose.'

It sounded so unlikely in her own ears she wondered if she'd gone too far, but Ryan seemed happy enough with her story.

'Then fell in the pool because he was feeling woozy,' he offered.

He said goodbye and left, far too eagerly, but at least his arrival at the property would look natural and shouldn't raise any alarms.

The direction of her thoughts made her shiver, but there was too much to be done to be brooding over things—or shivering! Check on Lucy first.

She raced across to the cottage, and found Lucy in the kitchen.

'I found some chicken pieces in the freezer and thought I'd cook the dinner,' she said.

Sarah looked at her, and felt her heart crack open at the forced smile on her daughter's pale face.

'I hope it's something that will keep. I want to be here with you, love, but half the town's been poisoned by hamburgers, Ken Griffiths has had a bad accident and a policeman who looks younger than you is holding the fort...'

'I'll be OK, Mum,' Lucy assured her. 'And I always cook something that will keep.' Her smile grew infinitesimally wider. 'Early childhood training, I guess.'

Sarah spared the time to give her a hug.

'I'll do a quick whizz through the wards to see everything's OK, parcel up some hamburger samples to go to town for testing and be right back,' she promised.

Lucy returned the hug, and Sarah knew that, although there were a lot more tears to be shed, her daughter's inner strength would eventually get her through her grief.

Over at the hospital she checked on Charlie first. Emmie had used sterile foam pads to prop his body so he could relax in sleep but not roll over onto his injured back. A carefully calibrated drip was feeding fluids into his veins, aimed at replacing plasma lost as the body rushed to the defence of the wounded tissues, while a catheter and bag recorded his urine output.

Monitoring it would enable her to increase or decrease the amount of fluid he was receiving, and testing of the urine, as well as blood samples, would help her check his recovery.

'I don't see why he should have a room to himself and

I'm in the ward,' Bessie grumbled as Sarah approached the town's oldest citizen.

'All the company bothering you?' Sarah asked her, waving her hand around the empty spaces of the women's ward. Everyone had wanted to be home for the celebrations. The place was deserted.

'I like the company usually,' Bessie admitted, and Sarah realised her complaint was merely making conversation. She was lonely in here on her own.

'Have you heard all about the festivities so far?' Sarah asked her.

Bessie nodded.

'Emmie told me about the posh party you were at. Said your policeman was back in town.'

'You've got a better memory than most people half your age,' Sarah told her, wondering what else Emmie had passed on. She hadn't seen her friend in the short time she'd been at the McMurrays'. How much had Emmie seen of her?

'And that young nurse, Lisa, told me all about everyone being poisoned at the fête.'

Everyone being poisoned at the fête?

The phrase lingered in Sarah's head as she visited the sole occupant of the 'men's' ward. Grant Russell, a jackeroo, was in traction for a broken pelvis after he'd fallen off his bike while mustering.

'Well, you're one young man who won't be dancing tonight,' she told him.

'And won't have any visitors either. Everyone's going to the ball.'

'Not quite everyone. I'll be here on duty and so will at least one sister and one nurse. We'll see you don't get lonely.'

'I bet it's an old sister and an old nurse,' he grumbled. 'All the young ones will be at the ball.'

And I'm an 'old doctor' in his eyes, Sarah realised, as

she headed for the lab and the bags of food she had to tackle.

Which brought her back to 'everyone being poisoned'?

But it couldn't have been deliberate. There was no reason for someone to deliberately sabotage the school fête.

Or any of the festivities planned for the weekend.

The idea that further incidents could happen all but brought on a panic attack.

Impossible!

She concentrated on the task at hand, pulling on gloves and opening each bag of foodstuff, taking samples, sealing them in small specimen containers then labelling and dating each one.

It reminded her of other labels she'd attached earlier in the day and she wondered how badly damaged those samples had been in the accident.

Tony answered that question for her when he arrived after she'd disposed of the remnants of the hamburger stall's foodstuffs.

'The seals on the two boxes were still intact so I sent them on,' he answered. 'For some reason Ken had strapped them into the rear seat, using the seat belts. If he'd slung them into the back of the vehicle, they could have been thrown out and smashed to smithereens or at least tumbled about enough to break glass and contaminate the samples.'

'How did you get back here?' Sarah asked him, hoping to hide how pleased she was to see him now her anxiety over the specimens had been allayed.

'Ambulance. A policeman I knew came out from Karunga so I handed over responsibility for the boxes to him. I told him about Ken hearing a shot and suggested he check the blown tyre carefully—perhaps send it to the city for forensic tests—then I travelled into town with the tow truck, picked up the ambulance and came home in it.'

Sarah wanted to ask if he'd seen Ken, and if the man

had said anything else, but she sensed Tony had told her all he intended telling.

'Lucy's cooking dinner,' she said instead, and saw the worry on his face lessen slightly.

'Good for her. How's everything else here?'

'Settled,' Sarah told him, 'but possibly only for the moment, so let's go across to the cottage while the going's good.'

As they crossed the courtyard she realised how easily he'd slipped back into her life, and how much for granted she was taking his continued presence.

'Don't you have to be somewhere? Aren't you minding your boss tonight?'

He stopped, as if her words had reined him back.

'I'll call him and explain about Ken's accident. I'll probably have to make an appearance at the ball, but if I phone my real police boss first I may be able to wangle a temporary assignment out here.'

He was frowning, no doubt mentally listing other things he had to do.

'Damn! I forgot about the tablets. James's belongings are still out at Craigmoor.'

Sarah knew her smile was probably smug as she touched his shoulder and said, 'That's one worry you don't have.' She related her conversation with Ryan.

Tony reached for her, taking her by the waist and swinging her around in the air before settling her, none too steadily, back on her feet.

'Don't we make a great team?' he demanded. 'Don't we?'

She was pleased his mood had lifted, but remembered why they were teamed and sobered immediately.

Let it be an accident, she prayed, as the thought of someone deliberately harming James was almost more than she could bear.

Tony must have caught her thoughts, for he responded by hugging her to him.

'I know how you feel,' he said gently. 'But, rest assured, we'll sort it out.'

He kissed the top of her head, and rubbed his hands up and down her arms.

'I'll be as short a time as possible at the ball,' he promised, 'and, as I told you earlier, I'll stay on in Windrush until we find out what happened to James, whatever it takes to do it.'

She lifted her head from his shoulder, intending to thank him, but the words were unsaid as once again his lips claimed hers and she gave herself up to physical delights she'd all but forgotten existed.

Bright lights played across them, and embarrassment broke them apart.

'It's Ryan,' Sarah muttered, recognising the police vehicle.

'Good. Let's see what he's got for us,' Tony said.

'Doesn't anything embarrass you?' Sarah demanded, following a few paces behind as he strode towards the now stationary car.

'A lot of things,' he admitted. 'But kissing you isn't one of them.'

It was a compliment, she realised, as she reached the vehicle, and saw Ryan hold a plastic bag aloft.

'I've got his overnight bag as well,' he said, 'but his toiletries are in here and I put the tablet bottle in this small bag.'

He passed the smaller bag to Tony.

'They weren't in the toilet bag, or anywhere in the room, but I stood my ground and said Ken had seen them earlier and had specifically asked me to bring them back to the station. Mrs McMurray began to cry and say she didn't want people thinking bad things about James, or upsetting her husband with gossip, so she'd taken them out and hidden them in with her own tablets.'

'Well done,' Tony told him. 'I'll take the tablets so the doc can have a look at them, then drop them back at the station later. You've written down what they are? Made a note of everything you took?'

'And photographed them,' the young man said proudly. 'I took shots of the room before I touched anything, and then I photographed the tablet bottle separately.'

He passed Tony the bag with the small white container in it. 'Good man!' Tony praised, but his attention was on the exhibit as he peered at it through the plastic.

'The label looks very tatty,' he said.

'Maybe it's an old prescription he had. Something for an allergy, or old antibiotics,' Sarah suggested, but when Tony passed it to her, she knew it wasn't going to be that easy.

She read the name and felt her stomach lurch uneasily. Could she have been so wrong in her judgement of James's mood? Could Lucy have been way off beam as well?

'What is it?'

Tony, perhaps sensing her despair, asked the question.

'It's a sedative. The brand name rings a bell. It's butobarbitone, I think, though I'd have to look it up in the pharmaceutical book because it's not something I regularly prescribe.'

'Prescribed to James?'

They were still standing by the car and she was examining it by the light from the cabin.

'I can't see it well enough to read the name here, although I'm sure it says McMurray.'

'We'll take it inside,' Tony suggested and, at that moment the police radio began to chatter.

Ryan listened, then said, 'Trouble at the pub. I have to go. What if I sign all this gear over to you? Will that satisfy chain of evidence requirements?'

'As I've been officially asked to help, I can't see why

not,' Tony told him, and Sarah waited while the seals on all the packages were signed to confirm the transfer.

Then she helped him carry the things towards the house, halting when she came to where light from the windows threw yellow squares across the grass.

'Let's dump all but the tablet bottle into your car and lock it,' she suggested, and Tony, guessing why she was reluctant to take James's belongings into the cottage, agreed.

Sarah went ahead into the house, one hand wrapped around the bottle in its small plastic bag.

Lucy was staring blankly at a noisy games show on the television. She looked up as Sarah came in.

'Is Tony with you? What has he found out?'

'Not much,' Sarah admitted. 'It's been a very disrupted day, one way or another.' She saw the disappointment on Lucy's face and wondered if asking for her assistance, rather than hiding things from her, might help her through the next few days.

'Did James ever take anything to help him sleep?' she asked.

Tony came in and Lucy ran to him, seeking comfort in his arms before replying to the question.

'Never!' She was adamant in her denial. 'He hated that sort of thing. Apparently Alana used to take sedatives on a regular basis. After James's mother died he had trouble sleeping, and Alana would mix bits of her tablets into milk to help him. Of course, he was often dopey the next day, and eventually Stewart found out what was happening and went into one of his "macho men don't need drugs" lectures. Back then, poor James was trying to do whatever he could to please his father, so that was that, as far as any drug experimentation was concerned.'

She moved away from Tony as she explained, then, seeing the bag in Sarah's hand, asked, 'Why?'

Sarah glanced at Tony, who nodded.

'This empty tablet bottle was in his toilet bag,' she explained. 'You can look at it through the plastic but that's all.'

Lucy took the bag and peered intently at it.

'The label's torn,' she said impatiently. 'It could belong to anyone. And if it's empty how would you know what's been inside it? Did you look, Tony? I often use these little bottles for moisturising cream when I don't want to carry a full jar of it.'

'A laboratory can test any remnants of dust or particles in it to see what was in there,' Sarah explained, as Lucy turned the package over in her hands then stretched the plastic across the label in an attempt to read it more clearly.

'Ken sniffed at it when he found it this morning,' Tony elaborated. 'There didn't appear to be anything moist like a cream in it but, as you say, he could have carried something else in it—aspirin, earplugs, anything small.'

Lucy didn't answer, but continued to examine the torn label closely.

'I suppose it got wet, being carried in with his toothbrush and razor, that's why the label's so shaggy, but…here.'

She handed the bag to her mother and headed for her bedroom, returning with a small chemist pack of tablets.

Sarah recognised what they were and her heart clenched for her daughter who'd put so much store in this one weekend, only to have it end in such sorrow.

'I went on them last month—for all the good it did me,' Lucy said, making a brave joke of her first venture into birth control. 'I'll probably die a virgin now!'

Tony reached for her and hugged her, murmuring comforting words, but although she nestled against him for a moment she soon pulled herself together.

'Look!' she said, pointing to the chemist's label on the outside of the box. 'Although the one on the bottle is very torn, there's enough of it to tell it's from the same chemist. See the dark blue here, and the name in yellow. I guess because the labels are printed and the prescription just typed on, the printed letters are more legible.'

'An Armidale chemist?' Sarah said, pleased Lucy was handling this so well, though she was intelligent enough to realise her discovery pointed to the contents of the bottle being a prescription made up for James.

'And his name's on it,' Lucy continued. 'Not only most of McMurray but there's the "a" of James as well.'

She looked expectantly at Tony who congratulated her then excused himself to make some phone calls, walking through to Sarah's bedroom to use his mobile.

Lucy waited until he'd disappeared, then flicked the package back to Sarah.

'Were they sedatives, Mum?' she asked, then added sadly, 'Doesn't say much for his level of excitement about the weekend if he thought he'd need to resort to sleeping tablets.'

Sarah dropped the plastic bag on the bench, then put her arms around her precious daughter and held her tight.

'Don't go leaping to conclusions. You're the one who pointed out the bottle could be an old one, a prescription he had years ago, perhaps when he was depressed early in his university course. Remember how he started Ag. Science to please Stewart and hated it so much it's a wonder he didn't give up on study for ever.'

Lucy nodded, then eased her body out of the embrace.

'It's a nice thought, Mum, but the date is legible. Six weeks ago. That's roughly when we first started talking about coming up to Windrush this weekend.'

'And probably before you started thinking about the sexual possibilities the weekend might offer,' Sarah pointed out. 'You said you had to persuade him to come. Maybe he thought sedation was the way to tackle it.'

Lucy looked at her, and Sarah could almost see her mind working.

'You think he might have taken an overdose of the tablets?' she asked gruffly. 'Taken his own life?'

'No, I don't,' Sarah said firmly, 'but other people will argue that way and we must be prepared to counter those arguments. We have to be prepared to stand by our conviction that James was on top of the world and so absorbed in his future there's no way he'd have taken his own life.'

'Thanks, Mum,' Lucy said, but she was blinking tears from her eyes as she spoke. 'I think I'll have my dinner later,' she mumbled, and, handkerchief in hand, she headed back into the bedroom she'd used as a child.

'Let her have her little cries,' Tony said, returning as Sarah watched the bedroom door close behind her daughter.

He tilted Sarah's chin and looked into her eyes.

'You could probably do with one yourself, but let's eat instead. I've begged off dinner with the Minister, but assured him I'll be back at the motel in time to change into a monkey suit and accompany him to the ball.'

Sarah read the regret in his eyes, but knew he had to do his job.

'I won't have to stay long,' he promised, dropping a quick kiss on her lips. 'If you'd like me to come back here...'

She shook her head, then said quickly, 'I don't mean no, I wouldn't like you to come back here, it's just—'

He smiled, folded his arms around her, and kissed her properly.

'Like Lucy, I can manage to stay celibate for a little longer,' he said gently. 'Come back here to put together what we have so far—that was all I meant.'

'I'd like that,' Sarah told him, not mentioning that she'd like other things as well. But there was no way she could re- embark on a love affair with Tony in the midst of her daughter's pain and heartache.

No way she could consider it, until they knew what had happened to James.

CHAPTER SEVEN

SARAH, feeling as uneasy as a teenager on a first date, served the chicken casserole Lucy had prepared. She wanted to avoid discussing James's death—at least until they'd eaten. Her mind needed a break from the constant theorising.

But what did you talk about to a man you hadn't seen for eleven years, yet once had known so intimately?

'You look fit, Tony. Do you still play tennis? Run?'

He chuckled, as if he guessed her dilemma, then came into the kitchen and stood behind her, looping his arms around her waist while she added mashed potatoes to the plates.

'It's hard, isn't it? Once we'd have been content to be silent, happy just to be together during the odd hours we could snatch from both our duties.'

He pulled her back towards him and hugged her tight.

'Yes, I still play tennis when I can get a game, and I run each morning. Age and having this sedentary office job makes that imperative.'

He kissed her neck then released her, carrying the loaded plates out to the dining area.

'The year we spent together was the happiest year of my life,' he said, holding her chair for her and speaking so matter-of-factly he could have been talking about the weather.

'Mine, too,' Sarah found herself admitting. Then, when he took his seat across the table from her, she smiled at him. 'Why did it all go so terribly wrong?'

'Stupid pride on my part, for a start,' he suggested. 'Immaturity as well. By the time I'd figured out what an ass

I'd been, going off in a huff when you questioned me about the rumours rather than battling it out, I was fifteen hundred miles away from you. And handling a job that was way beyond my capabilities.'

'I doubt that,' Sarah countered, but she knew he'd spent many years in a remote area where policing meant days and days of travel over excruciatingly bad roads, rescuing stranded adventurers from their own folly and ensuring the safety of the locals in that vast outback setting.

'It's the truth,' he said, 'but youth has other compensations. For one thing, you still believe you're immortal. Early in my time out there, I ran across three men in the national park who were trapping native birds and reptiles for export—part of a large smuggling gang. What I should have done was slink back to my office, contact the district headquarters for experts and support and wait while a plan was hatched to catch them.'

'By which time they could have got away,' Sarah suggested.

'My thoughts exactly,' he told her. 'So I went leaping in where anyone with any sense would have feared to tread, the three blokes shot off in two vehicles, which meant I couldn't follow both, leaving the trapped and drugged specimens behind for me to handle. Ever given mouth-to-mouth to a budgerigar?'

She chuckled at the question, although only seconds earlier she'd felt shock judder through her at the idea of him charging into danger.

He reached across the table and touched her hand.

'I adapted to the environment, learned how to use it to my advantage and how to do a better job. But it was definitely a bachelor posting. Not the kind of place I could have asked you and Lucy to share with me,' he added, his eyes no longer laughing at the memory. 'Also, I knew how much you loved your work, and by the time I was in a town big enough to have a hospital and a school for Lucy…'

'Yes?' she prompted.

'I was still caught up with the status thing. And in my more optimistic moments I figured it was too late to try to start again. I couldn't believe you wouldn't have met someone else. You were too easy to love for me to imagine you still single.'

'You always did have too low an opinion of your charm,' she teased, then she, too, grew serious. He'd talked about how he'd felt—now it was her turn.

'At first I was so confused—so hurt—I couldn't think straight. Then I got angry. That was better.'

'At me?'

She grinned at him.

'No, not at you. At myself. I felt I shouldn't have put myself in a position where the hurt could happen.' She held up her hand to silence his protest. 'Yes, I know! I eventually accepted it was a stupid reaction, because if you don't take risks in life you get nowhere. But it took a while for me to figure all that out.'

'And Lucy going off to boarding school? How did you handle that?'

She looked into his eyes and saw compassion and understanding.

'I cried for about a month—perhaps two! Well, no longer than a year!' she confessed. 'But I knew that to keep her with me would be selfish on my part. She wanted to go so badly. To her it was the ultimate adventure, and, with the unpredictable hours I worked, it even made sense. But I hated it. Blamed myself for being a bad mother—probably blamed you as well. You got the blame for all the bad stuff that happened in my life back then!'

He smiled and she forgot the past, the years they'd been apart. The conversation drifted back and forth, words to fill in the gaps in time.

'And after the remote posting, where did you go next?''

'Forgettable places mostly. It's a bit of a blur as I did a number of relieving jobs, interspersed with staff training courses, external studies at university, a stint in the big smoke, working crime, then a new promotion came and I was in back in the country.'

'Armidale?'

'Armidale! I'd only been there a couple of months when one of the junior officers told me I had this date to speak at a girls' school. I tried my darnedest to get out of it, told them I didn't do traffic instruction, and copped a lecture on there being more to policing than traffic instruction.'

He smiled, as if remembering, then the grey eyes danced as he said, 'Believe me, Sarah, I was more terrified of that engagement than I'd been approaching the poachers on my own. An assembly hall full of female children and teenagers? Apprentice women? With my track record?'

'I'm sure you charmed the lot of them,' she told him, and he laughed.

'I don't know about charming them. But I certainly gained their attention when Lucy shot up in her seat and shrieked, "That's my Uncle Tony!"'

'She was so pleased to see you,' Sarah recalled. 'Her next letters told of nothing else. First there was a phone call, informing me you had to be put on her acceptable visitors' list forthwith, then all I heard was Uncle Tony did this, said that, took us there. It made me wonder if she was more homesick than she'd said. If she perhaps regretted her decision.'

'Not a bit of it,' Tony assured her. 'The only reason she cultivated me was the kudos it gave her, being collected for an outing in a police car!'

Sarah chuckled. 'You were very kind to put up with her.'

'It meant a lot to me, too,' he said, then added softly, 'And it brought me news of you.'

'Is that all you wanted?' she asked, as the air between them stiffened with a new tension.

'No,' he said gravely, 'but by that time you were doing a series of locums down around the Snowy Mountains area, as far away as I'd been when I was in the north-west.'

'I was always at the beach house for school holidays,' Sarah reminded him. 'You could have visited us there.'

'And interrupt the precious time you and Lucy had together? You forget I knew how much your daughter meant to you. I did a month-long apprenticeship, winning Lucy, before you'd even kiss me!'

Sarah smiled at the memory, but she'd caught a hint of restraint in his voice and suspected there was more. She raised her eyebrows to prompt him, and waited.

'I was going to contact you—needed so badly to see you—but fate, which seems to have dogged us, once again intervened. I was called to Sydney to join the team investigating a series of murders...'

His voice trailed away and Sarah guessed it had been a case which had become notorious—the worse serial killings in Australia's history.

As he looked at her she saw the signs of strain deepening in his cheek and guessed the toll that grisly work had taken of so sensitive a man. She took his hand across the table and held it tightly.

'We had to catch him, Sarah. Had to concentrate on the case to the exclusion of all else. I know men who quit the force when it was over, and others who might never be the same again. Me? I closed myself off to the world around me, and my work became my life. There's a saying, ''Each man's death diminishes me.'' Well, as far as I was concerned, that man's crimes defiled me. It took me a while to put it all behind me—and took about five years out of my life.'

His fingers gripped hers then released them, as if the admission embarrassed him.

'It couldn't have helped but affect you,' she murmured. 'The senseless deaths of young people…' She shuddered, her thoughts switching from other people's children to her own child.

His fingers took up her hand again, he becoming the comforter.

'There is no way Lucy would have harmed a hair on James's head, and that includes badgering him so much he committed suicide. Young men do not kill themselves to avoid sex.'

'You're sure of that?' Sarah asked him, while a warmth unconnected with sex, or even attraction, washed through her.

'Quite sure.' He stood up and came around to massage her shoulders again. 'Now, stop torturing yourself with thoughts that somehow she could be blamed. It might take time, but in the end the police usually get the right man. That's something the court system has going for it—the onus of proving guilt. The general feeling is that it's better for eight guilty people to get away with something than for one innocent person to be unjustly punished.'

She eased away from his hands and stood up, turning to face him.

'I'm not too sure about the eight guilty walking free, but I'll put my faith in you.'

He kissed her lightly on the lips.

'Now she tells me!' he murmured, and stepped away, although she guessed it was as hard for him to do as it was for her to let him. She walked him to his car, then returned reluctantly to the house.

After stacking the dishes in the sink, she went to check on Lucy, quietly twisting the knob and easing the door open so she didn't wake her daughter.

'Look, Mum,' her daughter said, turning from the small desk on the far side of the room.

Pleased by the strength in Lucy's voice, Sarah crossed towards her.

'I didn't realise you'd taken that,' she muttered when she saw the police exhibit of plastic bag and tablet bottle on the desk. Then, as her head threw up the implications of this breach of evidence security, her heart skittered madly.

'You haven't opened it? Touched the bottle?' she demanded, and Lucy turned towards her, frowning ferociously.

'I'm not a total idiot, Mum,' she said. 'Of course I haven't touched it. And Tony knows I've handled the bag so my fingerprints should be on that. But look!'

Sarah told her heart to settle down again and tried to concentrate. Lucy was pointing to a copy of the label she'd drawn on a ruled foolscap notepad.

'I measured it and drew it to size, then copied all the writing you can still read on it. I might not have got these numbers right, but down here I've put the alternatives which might look the same.'

She pointed further down the pad to a series of three numbers, none of which meant anything to Sarah.

'It must be a code the chemist uses,' Lucy explained, tapping the label on her own prescription. 'If he could look it up on the computer, he could tell us who it was for.'

Sarah was delighted to find Lucy was thinking positively, so was doubly reluctant to squash her suggestion. However, it was better to be practical about things before they both got carried away.

'But why wouldn't it have been made up for James?' she asked, tentatively offering caution as an option.

'I just know it wasn't, Mum. Besides, look at this.'

She pointed to the area where the most damage had occurred, as if the label had been damp then rubbed against something else in the toilet bag until the typing was worn away.

'See! The first name is almost obliterated, except for the

lower case ''a'' in the middle of it. Then the McMurray is faint but clear enough to read.'

Sarah looked, but no blinding flash of inspiration struck her.

'James has an ''a'' in it,' she reminded her daughter, who gave a long-suffering daughterly sigh.

'I know it does, but it's closer to the beginning of the word. Look further up, where the chemist has typed the instructions. He, or she, used a single space between words. Now, if whoever typed it used the same single space between ''James'' and ''McMurray'', then the ''a'' is in the wrong place.'

She flipped a page on the pad and revealed three names printed one beneath the other.

James McMurray.

Alana McMurray.

Stewart McMurray.

'James has three letters after his ''a'', including an ''m'' which is a fat letter. I've written them as small as the typing and measured them. It doesn't work, Mum. The chemist must either have run the words of his name together or the prescription was made up for Alana or Stewart.'

Her voice intimated her mother could take her pick, and Sarah realised Lucy didn't care who had owned the tablet bottle found in James's room as long as he was exonerated and no lingering suspicion of suicide could taint his memory.

Or her memory of him.

What she might not have considered was that the elimination of suicide, if drugs *were* found in his system, brought the black shadow of murder into all their lives.

'But the script was made up in Armidale,' Sarah pointed out. 'Had either James or Alana visited James in recent months?

Lucy shrugged.

'James has been in Sydney so I wouldn't have seen them if they did come, but Alana and Stewart are usually in town for Wool Week. That was about six weeks ago. What we have to do is ask the chemist to look up the number—or the possible numbers. I could phone him now.'

Sarah put an arm around her shoulders and gave her a quick hug.

'Tony will organise it for you. It's better done officially and, speaking of officially, you shouldn't have this plastic bag, but I'm glad you did because it gives us a great starting point. Now, what about some food?'

Lucy shook her head, and Sarah realised the challenge of the pill bottle had buoyed her up. Now that had been put on hold, she was sinking fast.

Shock treatment?

Why not?

'Why would anyone want to harm James?' she asked. 'Either Stewart or Alana, if we're looking at them as prime suspects? Stewart wanted James to take over Craigmoor, but drugging him insensible, perhaps even killing him, wasn't going to achieve his aim. At least with James alive, there was always a chance he'd change his mind.'

She didn't add that having the tablets suggested premeditation, not an act of sudden rage or anger following an argument.

Lucy spun around in the chair and gazed unseeingly over Sarah's right shoulder.

'There's no reason,' she admitted reluctantly. 'None that I can fathom. I mean, it isn't as if Alana had a child and wanted to cut James out of the inheritance. And, as you say, it made things worse, if anything, for Stewart. Except that Stewart isn't a man who likes being crossed. James didn't say much, but I know he—I suppose feared is too strong a word, but he had a lot of trepidation about facing his father.'

'Let's get off family,' Sarah suggested. 'Look at friends.

James has had girlfriends in the past. Could your new relationship with him have stirred someone to such anger?'

Lucy barely considered it, before replying. 'Marion Curtis might have poisoned me—she always hated me and my friendship with James—but she wouldn't have harmed him.' She shuddered, as if the reality of his death had struck her yet again. 'I rang Rosie and asked her to tell our close friends. They'll all come up. We might stay at the pub rather than here. Would you mind, Mum?'

'No, love,' Sarah said gently, knowing Lucy was at an age when friends would do more to help her through the tragedy than her mother could. Which reminded her of people she must tell—her own parents to begin with, who'd grown to love James nearly as much as they loved Lucy.

A familiar bar of a Bach melody—the call mode set for Lucy's mobile—halted their conversation. Lucy answered and Sarah left the room, pleased her daughter had friends who would grieve with her and support her through this time.

Although she should eat as well.

She heated a small bowl of chicken casserole in the microwave and took it back into the bedroom, leaving it on the desk where Lucy might pick at it as she listened to her friends' condolences. She retrieved the plastic bag and peered at the torn label. Was Lucy right? Had this script been made up for someone else and left in James's toilet bag to make his death look like an accidental overdose or suicide?

According to Stewart, Alana had enough pills to stock a pharmacy. She would be the most likely person to have a script for sedatives.

But hadn't Ryan said she'd taken the bottle and hidden it among her own?

Why put it there, then take it away? It made no sense.

Unless she took it to protect Stewart.

'I'm not so sure,' Tony said, as Sarah relayed her inconclusive maze of conjecture to him later. He'd arrived much earlier than she'd expected, looking so handsome in his dinner suit that her heart had gone haywire again.

A discussion of murder had seemed a good way of handling her own weakness.

He smiled, nodded to indicate, yes, he'd like a coffee, then took off his jacket and undid his bow tie. He removed the top stud of his dress shirt, and managed to look even more devastating.

'On the strength of that alone,' he told her, apparently oblivious to her near-swooning state, '*you're* ready to absolve her of any wrong-doing and, what's more, if her prints are found on the toilet bag or the bottle she now has a rational explanation for them being there.'

'But if this was planned, and the existence of the bottle suggests it was, she'd have had enough sense to have worn gloves when she planted it. Six-year-old children know about fingerprints, and not to leave them at the scene of a crime.'

Tony sighed.

'I agree with you that if the bottle proves a plant, whoever put it there would probably have worn gloves, although being caught wandering around the house in gloves might have proved awkward. But, as I see it, the problem would have been getting James's prints on it.'

'That's easy,' Sarah told him, bringing over to him coffee and some biscuits Emmie had dropped in. 'If it was Alana, she could have said the lid was stuck and asked him to open it for her. Or got him to read the label—she couldn't find her glasses. I can think of a number of ways to get someone's prints on something.'

He grinned at her, which did nothing to aid the regaining of her equilibrium.

'Please, don't take up a life of crime,' he warned. 'I'd hate to have to double guess the convoluted workings of your mind.'

Once again Sarah felt the warmth of companionship flow through her blood and realised how much she'd missed it, but warmth and companionship weren't going to solve the puzzle of James's death. She forced her mind to focus on practicalities.

'You said the bottle was empty when Ken found it this morning,' she began, squashing her physical reactions to this man with a common-sense approach. 'So we're supposing whoever planted it—Lucy's mysterious intruder—had already fed James the drugs and put it there to suggest he'd taken them.'

'So, not realising how things stood with Lucy, going into James's room wasn't particularly risky?' Now it was Tony who was staring off into the distance as he mused on the problem. 'We need Ken's notebook to confirm it, but I'm sure a couple of the guests he interviewed mentioned seeing James asleep by the pool towards the end of the evening,' he said eventually.

'And Lucy saw him there earlier,' Sarah confirmed. 'It's where they argued over the cup of coffee.'

Tony must have seen her shiver, for he stood up and took her in his arms. 'It's OK. She didn't drink the coffee.'

'I know—but if she had!'

'Who made the coffee? Do you know that?'

'Stewart!' Sarah told him, pleased to have at least one answer, although the abrupt transition startled her. 'That much I do know because James and Lucy had an argument about it. James proclaimed it a symbol, saying it was one of the rare times his father had done something for him.'

'But if James was by the pool, how did he know his father actually *made* it? OK, so he handed it to the lad, but someone in the kitchen may have poured it, another someone could have added sugar if he took it. Was it left lying about on a table or bench where anyone could have slipped in powdered sedatives? Was it specifically made for James? Could it have been made for Stewart, and his act of handing it over to James made the gesture more meaningful to James—explained the symbolism?'

Sarah groaned.

'I want fewer questions, not more of them. What puzzles me is the fact that no cup with his prints on it was found by the pool.'

Tony rested his hands on her shoulders.

'That makes it nasty. The tablets being in his room point us towards him taking them deliberately. Swallowing them whole with a glass of water. If that had happened, James's coffee-cup would have had nothing but coffee in it so could have been left with all the others.'

Sarah thought it through. 'The dirty cups puzzled me from the beginning, just the fact that they were there at all. But if we're looking at a careful staging of a suicide, per-haps the cups were left for us to find and test, including one near the lounge where James was sleeping. If someone did drug him, he or she was clever enough to know we might test the dregs in all the cups but didn't think about the police printing them all.'

'Especially not if there was pressure from the family to rule it an accident!' Tony gave her shoulders a gentle squeeze, then steered her towards a chair. 'Would it have to have been murder that was planned? I know we're gal-loping ahead here and presupposing the labs will find drugs, but if he hadn't somehow gone into the pool what would have happened? Would he have slept off the drug?'

Sarah frowned as she considered the question.

'It depends on the dosage. In fact, because drugs with the potential to kill are only doled out in safe quantities, people who want to kill themselves have to save up several lots of prescriptions over a period of months and then take them all at once.'

'So let's assume it was deliberate and James was the chosen victim. If doping him wasn't going to kill him—if the plunge into the pool was planned from the beginning—

wasn't it all a bit risky? What if he went to sleep some-where else? The plot fails.'

Sarah considered this for a few moments.

'Not if he habitually lay by the pool late at night. With the wheels on those long sun-lounges, there'd be nothing easier than to tip a heavily drugged person into the water—and without leaving any trace of what had happened.'

'You're a genius. It worried me that his shoes weren't scuffed—he certainly hadn't been dragged. I've been con-sidering someone strong enough to lift him—or two people working together, which is always risky.'

They had settled into two worn but comfortable arm-chairs and were batting their ideas back and forth across the coffee-table. Once again, Sarah felt a sense of ease in Tony's presence—a reassurance—although her heart ached for James and her mind was bogged down with unanswer-able questions.

'What if he hadn't fallen asleep by the pool?' Tony asked. 'Would the murderer have given up, do you think?'

Sarah considered.

'We're leaping a long way ahead, even believing there might be a murderer, but I've recently seen a case where an elderly lady was smothered while she slept. *If* James drank drugged coffee, then, feeling tired, went to bed, he could have been smothered in a similar way. Death results from anoxia in both drowning and smothering. It's caused by a lack of oxygen to the brain. If, as I suspect, he was so deeply drugged he didn't wake and struggle in the pool, I doubt he'd have fought an attacker who held a pillow or a thin sheet of plastic over his mouth and nose.'

'So where does the wound on his head come into it? Could he have bumped his head on the edge of the pool as he was tipped in?'

'I wouldn't think so,' Sarah replied. 'If the weight of his body was behind an accidental knock, I would have ex-pected more damage.'

She shivered, and Tony stood up and moved to perch on the arm of her chair and put an arm around her shoulders.

'It's all supposition,' he reminded her. 'So, out with it.'

She looked up into his eyes and saw his concern for her, and in that moment wanted him so badly the tragedy was all but wiped from her mind.

But the possibility that someone had cold-bloodedly killed so clever, charming and lovable a young man as James put a brake on her emotions.

'If someone wanted to make it look like an accident, a mark on his head would be a pointer in that direction. Perhaps if it hadn't been James—if Lucy hadn't been involved—I would have accepted the suggestion of accidental death and not done as thorough an autopsy. Particularly with pressure from the family—not to mention the Police Minister—to go along with an acceptable solution. I'm sure Ken Griffiths wouldn't have pushed me to do more.'

'Yes, Stewart certainly blew his top about the investigation,' Tony reminded her, then he turned as they heard the bedroom door open and Lucy appeared.

'That was Rosie. They're already on their way, driving through the night. They'll be here early in the morning.' Lucy made these announcements as she entered the living room.

She deposited the small bowl—empty, Sarah was pleased to see—on the divider and headed straight for Tony.

He shifted back into an armchair and took her on his knee—exactly as he had when she'd been seven and they'd sat in the same chair together.

'Did Mum tell you about the label?' she asked.

He glanced at Sarah across her shoulder, raised his eyebrows, then shook his head.

'I'll get my notes to show you,' she said, leaping off his knee and disappearing into the bedroom.

'She worked it out herself—it's worth following up. And

while she's explaining I'll slip across to the hospital and check that all's quiet over there.'

She glanced at her watch and saw it was close to eleven.

'Will you still be here when I get back?'

He smiled, then shook his head.

'Mentioning the label reminded me I have to get the bottle sent off to the lab. I'll send the toilet bag as well. There should be evidence of the label damage in it—if it happened naturally. I'll pack everything up and put it on tonight's bus. It'll be in the city by midday tomorrow.'

He stood up and came towards her, kissing her lightly on the lips.

'I'll see you in the morning. Take care.'

CHAPTER EIGHT

As Sarah walked out the door she heard Lucy speak to Tony, and, after seeing the pair's closeness, felt a twinge of regret that she'd denied Lucy a father figure.

Although it hadn't been entirely her fault. After all, the stories about Tony and Anna had been convincing. And her anguished reactions of pain, anger and bewilderment had made rational thinking impossible.

As she entered the hospital, dimly lit this time of night, she tried to put the puzzles of the past behind her. There was enough mystery in the present to keep her mind more than occupied. Once they'd sorted out what had happened to James, she and Tony could revisit that time—perhaps try to work out how the stories had begun.

Or where they'd begun.

The hospital was quiet, and Sarah made her way to Outpatients, where the nurse on duty was reading a travel magazine.

'I've often longed for a night shift when nothing happened, but now I've got one I'm bored to death,' she told Sarah. Then she cocked her head to one side as they heard a car pull up outside. 'Maybe I spoke too soon.'

A man in his mid-thirties came in, half supporting and half carrying an older woman.

'It's my aunt,' he explained. 'I think she might have eaten whatever made people sick at the school fête but had a delayed reaction. She's got terrible pains.'

Sarah and the nurse helped him lift the pale and sweating woman onto an examination table, where she curled herself into a tight ball.

'I'm Sarah Gilmour and this is Susie Curtis.' Sarah introduced herself and the nurse. 'I need to have a look at you, ask a few questions. Are you up to it?'

The woman nodded but stayed curled up.

'Her name's Clare Rose,' the nephew said, as Susie worked a blood-pressure cuff around their patient's arm. 'She's come down to stay with her sister, my mother, for the celebrations and now this has happened.'

'Where's the pain?' Sarah asked, and Mrs Rose pressed her hand to her right upper abdomen.

'It goes around my back and into my shoulder,' she said, and began to shiver.

'Have you ever had problems with your gall bladder?' Sarah asked, pressing gently over a palpable mass just under the border of the liver and withdrawing her hands as the patient flinched and sucked in her breath.

'I've had the pain before, but not this bad,' Mrs Rose explained, when she'd recovered enough to speak. 'The first time I rested and it went away. I didn't go to a doctor to find out what it was.'

She winced as she moved, then curled up again, while Susie passed the thermometer to Sarah to show a temperature of 40 degrees Celsius. To Sarah it made an infection like cholecystitis more likely than gallstones.

'It's definitely centred in your gall bladder,' Sarah told her. 'The first time you had the pain it may have been a gallstone passing into the duct, and, although it finally got through and the pain stopped, this could be an infection resulting from that.'

She spoke to Susie, who hurried off to find an orderly, then explained to the patient, 'I'll X-ray you first, although not all gallstones show up on X-ray. If no other complication is revealed, we'll take it from there.'

When the orderly arrived they wheeled the patient into the X-ray room, where Sarah, used to doing all the jobs in a small hospital, took two films, one upright—a position Mrs Rose found extremely uncomfortable—and one supine.

'It helps eliminate other possibilities,' she told the patient as she snapped first one, and then the second film into the light-box. No signs of a perforated ulcer, but no radio-opaque gallstones either.

After giving Mrs Rose the 'good news, bad news' scenario, Sarah said, 'I'll have to keep you in hospital. I'll get a drip started to get some fluids flowing into your blood, and give you something for the pain. Once you're comfortable, we'll talk about your options.'

She called the orderly and sent him with Susie to settle the patient into a bed, while she returned to Outpatients to speak to the nephew.

'She'll need to be hospitalised for at least a few days,' she explained. 'I'll give her a special dye in her drip tonight, then tomorrow X-ray her again to see what shows up.'

'Can't you zap gallstones now? Or melt them with acid? Get rid of them without surgery?'

'A specialist in the city might be able to break them up, using keyhole surgery and a specialised tool, and there are drugs that can "melt" them, but up here we don't have such great technology. Even in the city, she'd have to have the X-rays to see if stones are present and further tests. I think it's more likely to be an infection. That's a different thing altogether and requires bed rest and hospital care for a few days whether surgery is performed or not.'

He nodded as if satisfied, and then walked through to the ward with Sarah to say goodbye to his aunt.

'Could you bring my suitcase up?' she asked him. 'I didn't unpack so all my night things are still in it.'

'I'll be right back,' he assured her, and hurried out, giving Sarah the impression he was missing out on celebrations somewhere.

Explaining what she was doing, she inserted a needle into Mrs Rose's arm and attached the drip tubing.

'Are you allergic to any drugs?' Susie asked, reaching

that part of the patient form she'd been completing while Sarah had been speaking to the nephew.

'Not allergic to anything,' Mrs Rose replied.

'What about tablets? Are you on any drugs for blood pressure, arthritis, anything at all?'

'No drugs, no tablets. I'm healthy, apart from this pain.'

Sarah was reassured, deciding to use pethidine to ease the pain and help Mrs Rose relax, and to start antibiotic therapy to fight the infection in the woman's body.

Take blood first. Step by step Sarah worked through the process of diagnosis and treatment. Mary Thomas, the night sister, joined her in the ward, assisting while Susie returned to her post in Outpatients.

It was another hour before Sarah was satisfied she'd completed the simple blood tests and done all she could for her patient. Then, grateful no other late night emergencies had arisen, she crossed the yard between the rear of the hospital and the cottage, sudden exhaustion reminding her how long the day had been.

A sad day, too, she remembered as she checked on Lucy then crawled gratefully into bed.

Now she had time to think of James and grieve his loss. Memories knotted in her chest, and she shed quiet tears into the pillow. Then, after a silent vow to him that she would find the truth, she forced her body to relax and willed her mind to stop thinking, using techniques she'd mastered over many years to drift into sleep.

'I don't do mornings!' Sarah mumbled at the intruder who kept shaking insistently at her shoulder. 'Come back later. Tomorrow. Next week.'

'That's not a nice welcome for your lover at the break of day,' a deep voice murmured.

Sarah shoved her head further under the pillow.

'I don't have a lover, and even if I did I wouldn't want him hanging around this early.'

She felt lips move on her shoulder, the back of her neck, then a husky whisper ask, 'Would you like a lover?'

'Not before I've cleaned my teeth and washed my face,' she grumbled. Then she remembered something else and added, 'And had a cup of coffee.'

'I've done the coffee. Pull your head out from under there and smell.'

She emerged reluctantly and frowned at Tony, freshly washed and shaven, neatly clad, looking far too alive for what—six in the morning?

'Go away!' she muttered at him, but she shuffled into a half-sitting position, took the coffee he offered her and breathed deeply to inhale the revivifying aroma.

'I will—I am. That's what I came to tell you.'

'What do you mean?' she yelped, sitting straighter and spilling coffee everywhere.

'A big hook's come out and yanked me back to Sydney,' he said gravely. 'I had a message from the Commissioner himself when I returned to the motel last night. I can't not go, Sarah, but I'll be back as soon as possible. I may even do some good down there. Chase up whoever's handling the lab work and get the results a bit faster.'

Sarah set the coffee carefully down on the bedside table, glared at Tony and muttered, 'Don't you dare leave until I get back!'

She darted out of bed and hurried to the bathroom.

Perhaps with her hair brushed, face washed and teeth cleaned, she'd be better able to assimilate this latest shock.

'You're going back to Sydney?' she said as she walked back into the bedroom to find he'd stripped off the coffee-stained sheets and bundled them up on the end of the bed.

'Not for long,' he assured her, and came forward to take her in his arms.

Her body slumped against him, aching with denial, and when his lips met hers she knew there was too much hunger in her kiss—too much need for him to be there for her, joined with other needs his re-emergence in her life had generated.

'I'll be back within a day or two,' he promised.

'You can't be if you're driving down,' she pointed out, and he hugged her closer.

'Driving to Tamworth and flying from there. Believe me, Sarah, darling, I will be back as soon as I possibly can be, even if I have to flap my arms and fly myself.'

Sarah, darling?

She held on tighter, afraid of losing him again and scared to face the future—even a day or two of it—alone.

'You'll manage,' he whispered, pressing kisses on her cheek and temple. 'Because you're strong, and Lucy needs you, and because I love you and have faith in you. Isn't that enough to keep you going?'

Sarah nodded her head against his shoulder, then shook it because she was tired of being strong, and being there for Lucy and battling on alone. Then Tony eased her away from him and looked into her eyes with so much love shimmering in his that she felt it jolt through her like an electric charge.

'I'll be thinking of you every minute,' he promised. 'Here with you in spirit if not in flesh. You *will* be strong, Sarah, because being strong is such an integral part of what you are. As much as silky soft, red-gold hair, and eyes that go hazy when I kiss you.'

His lips claimed hers, as if to prove his point, and she felt her body come alive as grief, and misery, and loneliness were banished by a kiss.

But only temporarily!

Minutes later, she stood in the doorway of the cottage and watched him drive away. Then the sound of another car broke the morning stillness. It clattered to a halt behind the screen of trees between the hospital and the cottage and disgorged four weary and dishevelled young people. Lucy's friends had arrived.

She greeted them warmly, shed tears with Rosie and Jill, hugged the two young men, who were known as Nod and Winkle for reasons Sarah had never fathomed, then led them all into the house for food and drinks.

'Very fetching house attire, Dr G.,' Nod remarked, and she realised she was still in her nightdress, a simple shift of fine white cotton, sheer enough to show her shape every time she stood in front of the window.

She left them in charge of toast-making and headed for her bedroom, puling on jeans and a T-shirt as a more practical alternative. Lucy had joined them by the time she returned, and was sobbing her heart out in Rosie's arms. The other three were making soothing noises interspersed with wisecracks about what James would and wouldn't allow in the way of grieving.

Yes, friends were what Lucy needed at the moment. Sarah left them together and crossed to the hospital, anxious to check on Mrs Rose and begin the next stage of diagnostic tests.

'It's been very quiet since you left,' Mary assured her. 'Mrs Rose slept right through and Bessie has announced she's well enough to go to the ecumenical church service in the park so Mrs French, the minister's wife, is coming up to collect her and take care of her. We'll be down to the emptiest hospital I've ever known.'

'Don't get too excited,' Sarah warned. 'Aren't they following the church service with a rodeo and camp draft? If we don't get patients out of that, I'll be surprised.'

'Sprains and bruises. Cissy stuff!' Mary teased, and Sarah smiled. Mary was one of the contestants in the women's events.

'Just remember that when your horse sends you flying over his head and you land on your rear end,' she warned, and Mary chuckled.

Then she grew grave, facing up to Sarah as if she had something important to relay.

'How's Lucy? I saw young people drive past the hospital and assume they are her friends. James's friends, too, I suppose. What a dreadful thing to happen to such a nice young man.'

'Yes, it was,' Sarah agreed, but she doubted whether Mary had heard her for she'd already launched into the next part of her conversation.

'That someone so young, with everything ahead of him, could kill himself. *Was* he gay? Is that why he and Stewart didn't get on? I mean, imagine Stewart having to cope with a son who wasn't one hundred per cent Aussie male! I couldn't believe it when I heard it. Such a hard road for young people to travel—not that it's their fault, of course, but—'

'Couldn't believe when you heard *what*?' Sarah broke into the flow, so astounded she thought she must have been mistaken. 'That James was gay? Who told you that? Who's spreading these stories?'

Even as she asked the questions her stomach cramped and she had to battle surging nausea. Stories, rumours. The past was no longer haunting her, but imprinting itself on the present.

Mary stepped back as if Sarah's sharp demands had struck her.

'I'm sorry, I shouldn't have been repeating gossip, but although I had to leave the ball early my husband Jeff stayed on, then came up to have a late supper or early breakfast with me a couple of hours ago. He said people were talking as if they'd always known, and now accepted it as the reason for his suicide.'

Sarah clamped her lips shut. Much as she wanted to shriek to the heavens that James had *not* committed suicide, she knew she had no proof of how he'd died and to say something at this stage could prove disastrous.

She eased them open enough to say, 'James was not gay. In fact, he and Lucy have been lovers for years.'

Which wasn't true, of course, but once that story spread it might stop the other rumours. She crossed her fingers behind her back and prayed Lucy would understand her motivation.

'You don't think that was a front? To show people he was normal?'

Sarah sighed. Obviously some rumours would be harder to scotch than others. She tried again.

'Not all people connected with the theatre are gay,' she pointed out. 'And it's only folk who don't know much about that life who'd believe such a rumour.'

And if that offended Mary, well, too bad.

'I wonder how it started?' she said, obviously not offended.

Sarah shrugged. 'How do any rumours start?'

She thought of the title of a short play James had been writing—*Chinese Whispers*. Gossip began and changed shape and form as it passed from person to person until it was so entirely restructured as to be unrecognisable.

But extremely dangerous.

'Perhaps you can start a new one spreading,' she told Mary, 'although if you can keep Lucy out of it I'd be grateful.'

'I understand,' Mary said, then she patted Sarah on the shoulder and walked away.

Sarah began with Mrs Rose, who was awake and apparently comfortable as she was sitting up in bed, arranging photos on the small bedside locker.

'I like to have my own things around, even if I'm not staying long,' she explained to Sarah. 'Are you going to X-ray me again now?'

'I guess we should get it over and done with,' Sarah told her. 'If there are stones, you might need to see a surgeon or specialist, but in the meantime we'll keep you here and give your gall bladder a rest—first by keeping you on a drip, then changing you onto a low fat diet and seeing how your body reacts to it.'

'I could do with the diet,' Mrs Rose told her, patting her ample belly.

Sarah checked her chart, made a note to decrease pain relief and lengthen the time between obs, then asked the nurse on duty to arrange for Mrs Rose to be wheeled through to X-Ray.

The X-ray showed a few small stones in the gall bladder—a common occurrence—but nothing obstructing the bile duct. It reinforced Sarah's opinion that it was an infection rather than a blockage. She'd have to check on where Mrs Rose lived and refer her on to someone nearer to her home.

When her patient had been wheeled backed to the ward, Sarah walked through the hospital, stopping to talk to her meagre supply of patients, pausing by Charlie's bed to check on the open wounds where she'd cut away the blistered skin.

Protocol for burns changed so often and so quickly that she was never certain if she was doing the right thing, but recent research suggested that prostaglandins in the fluid in the blisters promoted deeper burning. Since she'd begun the practice of cutting off the skin of the larger blisters and keeping the area clean and dry she'd had success, so stuck to it. At least, until something more effective was suggested!

Carey was with her son, reading him a story about a very hungry caterpillar. The child's eyes were bright but healthily so, not feverish, and his obs suggested that the burns had had little effect on his system.

'I'll take him off the drip at lunchtime,' she told Carey, then she squatted down so she could speak directly to Charlie.

'How do you feel?'

'My back hurts.'

The small pink bottom lip trembled at this admission.

'Yes, I know it does,' Sarah said softly. 'But it should be better soon. And hurting means it's getting better. It's a funny thing, but really bad burns don't hurt as much but they could keep you in hospital for weeks and weeks. So, really, you've been very lucky!'

'That's what Nan says,' Charlie told her. 'Can I listen to your chest?'

He pointed to the stethoscope protruding from Sarah's pocket, and she realised he knew the routine of the hospital well from previous visits.

She pulled it out and put the earpieces over his ears, then held the chestpiece with its bell and diaphragm to her chest.

'Hear anything?'

'A slushing noise.'

'Wonderful! That means I'm still alive.'

She detached the instrument, then studied him a moment longer.

'This stethoscope is a new one my daughter Lucy gave me last Christmas. I have my old one over at the cottage. Would you like to have it?'

'Is it real—like this one?' her patient demanded. 'Mum bought me one once but it was only a toy and you couldn't hear anything at all.'

'It's real, and I'll drop it over to you later,' Sarah promised him. 'You can check on your brothers and sisters when they come in.'

'I've only got one brother,' Charlie told her. 'He's going to be a farmer like Dad, but I'm going to be a doctor.'

'Well, you're certainly getting to know your way around a hospital,' Carey told him, but she ruffled his hair in a fond manner and Sarah felt a spurt of envy.

Lucy needed so little from her these days—they were more like friends than mother and daughter. To have another child—perhaps a little boy...

With eyes like polished steel?

She shut away the image, said goodbye to Carey, promised Charlie she'd be back and left the room before she could become too sentimental.

Tony might have called her darling, but one darling didn't make their future together a certainty. Especially after eleven long years apart.

And neither of them were young, so starting a family…

'Don't even think about it,' she muttered to herself, and ran slap bang into Graham who was wheeling Bessie out onto the verandah. Mrs French might be taking her to the service, but it was hospital policy that staff were responsible until the patient left the premises.

'Coming to the church service?' the old lady asked Sarah.

'I doubt I'll be busy here so I'll definitely be there for some of it,' she promised. After all, if Lucy didn't need her support she might as well be out in the fresh air and giving thanks for various small mercies.

Like her happy memories of James!

The service was pleasant and relaxed, and Sarah, who'd joined Emmie and her family on a blanket in the shade of a camphor-laurel tree, felt a sense of peace steal over her. Perhaps, for the rest of the day, she could forget about the mystery and just mourn James in a normal manner, thinking about the happy days at the beach, his habit of always bringing her a poem or a small posy of flowers when he visited, telling her they were better than chocolates, food for the soul and totally non-fattening.

She wiped away a tear as the final hymn ended, but the peace remained. Until she saw Stewart and Alana heading purposefully towards her. Given the mood Stewart had been in at their last meeting, a repetition was something she'd rather have avoided.

However, he was apparently back in control for he smiled and held out his hand. He asked after Lucy, then

said gruffly, 'I'd like her to have James's car. It's out at
the house. If you could drive her out some time to collect
it I'd be grateful—sad memories, looking at it all the time.'

Sarah was so flabbergasted by this expression of sorrow
she barely took in the offer.

'Perhaps this afternoon,' Alana suggested. 'We won't be
there but the keys are in it. Much as we'd like to be alone
to grieve for James, we have our duties to consider. We'd
agreed to take the Minister to the rodeo, and Stewart feels
we should keep to that.' She paused, and Sarah thought she
looked strained and tired—not altogether happy with her
husband's stiff-upper-lip approach.

Was she always so biddable? Going along with all his
decrees?

And why?

She realised they were waiting for her to say something
so she thanked them both, although she wondered how
Lucy would feel about the offer.

Perhaps she could look on it as a gift from James?

Perhaps!

Back at the cottage, she found the place deserted, a note
from Lucy explaining they'd all decamped to the hotel.

Not wanting to put it off until thinking about it made it
seem too difficult a task, she drove across to the hotel and
found the small group in a huddle over a table in the beer-
garden. With soft drinks in front of them, she noted with
approval. Talk would help them through their sorrows more
effectively than alcohol.

She sat down and explained Stewart's offer, but when
Lucy shuddered, and her eyes again filled with tears, Sarah
knew she'd made a mistake.

'It's OK, Luce!' Winkle put an arm around Lucy's shoulders and tucked her up against his manly chest. 'If the old
codger can't bear the sight of his son's car untidying his
garden, one of us will go out and retrieve it.'

'I'll go!'

Rosie was on her feet so quickly that Sarah guessed she either wanted to get away from the group for a while or had something to say to her.

'Thanks, Rosie. Is now OK with you?'

The girl nodded and grabbed the little knapsack slung across the back of her chair.

'See you guys later,' she said, and walked away.

Sarah had little choice but to touch Lucy on the head in farewell and follow her.

'Did we do the right thing, Dr G., coming up like this? I didn't like taking Lucy away from you like we did, because you loved him as much as the rest of us did, but she seemed to want to be with us.'

Sarah caught up with her and gave her a hug, then kept an arm around her shoulders as they walked to her car.

'You did exactly the right thing,' she assured her, 'and it will help her through it, having all of you around.'

Rosie smiled, then, when they were both strapped in and Sarah was heading out of town again, she brought up another question.

'I've copies of James's latest play in my bag. You know, the one-act thing he was working on for the competition. It's called *Chinese Whispers*, and it's still in draft form, but the basis of it is there. The four of us talked about it on the drive out here, and we thought we'd like to do a read-through of it at his funeral—or after it, outside the church. It's good—probably the best thing he'd written—but now it won't ever be finished, so it seemed…'

Sarah swallowed the huge lump that had formed in her throat. These brash young people could show such sensitivity at times that it never failed to astound her.

'I think it would be a great idea,' she said, framing the words with difficulty as the lump refused to go away. 'Have you mentioned it to Lucy?'

Rosie shook her head and her dark curls bounced.

'No. That's what I wanted to ask you. How do you think she'd feel about it?'

Maybe mothers did still have a place in teenage daughters' lives!

Or did they?

'I've no idea,' she admitted. 'The only way you'll find out is to ask. It's a tribute to James's talent so she shouldn't have any objection, but if she's been through the writing of it with him, been a sounding-board for him, it might bring back too many painful memories.'

Again the dark curls bounced.

'James never talked about his work as he was writing it. Not even to Luce! He said that once he'd talked about it he felt as if he'd already told the story so didn't need to write the play. I've only got a copy because he lent me his laptop when he went away and I noticed the file in there. When Lucy phoned, I opened it up and skimmed through it—realised how close to finished it was. That's when I had the idea. I printed off six copies because there are six parts.'

She looked hopefully at Sarah.

'I'm not committing myself to anything,' Sarah said firmly, but if she could honour James's memory in this way she knew she would.

'I'll drop one of the copies in to you when we've talked to Lucy about it,' Rosie promised, then began to talk about her course, as if that was enough discussion of James for the moment.

The little dark blue Toyota was sitting all alone on the front drive, and Rosie, having surveyed the sprawling house and the spacious gardens surrounding it, muttered, 'Well, I can understand them wanting it moved. It does seem out of place in all this splendour.'

Then she sighed.

'Poor James! He had such a strong genetic urge to do the right thing by everyone that his rebellion—in wanting to write, not work the land—caused him a lot of anguish.'

The words disturbed Sarah.

'How much anguish?' she demanded, and Rosie, apparently surprised by the abruptness of her demand, spun to face her.

'Not enough to kill himself.' Rosie rejected the idea out of hand. They remained in the car as if neither of them was willing to get out and walk towards James's treasured vehicle.

'There's a particularly nasty rumour going around town. You're likely to hear it,' Sarah began cautiously.

Rosie looked at her and nodded to signal she could cope.

'That James was gay and so ashamed of it he took his own life.'

To Sarah's surprise, Rosie not only took it well but she chuckled.

'None of his friends are going to believe that. James didn't make a secret of being attracted to women, even before the balance of his and Lucy's relationship shifted. And even if he had been gay, that stuff doesn't matter to people any more, Dr G. No one would kill himself over it. Well, not that alone.'

Sarah absorbed this information. Lucy's declaration about her virginity had surprised her—not so much the fact that her daughter hadn't had an affair by the time she was nineteen, but that she would talk so openly about it. When she'd been that age—younger, in fact, for her affair with David had begun at seventeen—she would no more have told her parents than she'd have announced it over the airwaves. Until she'd had to, of course.

Maybe Lucy wouldn't have mentioned it either if James hadn't died.

'I guess we'd better get back to town,' she said, and opened the car door so she could walk across with Rosie and also check that the keys *were* in the vehicle.

'Do you feel OK about this? Driving James's car back to town?'

Rosie smiled at her.

'I'll be fine,' she assured Sarah. 'But I think it would be better to leave it parked near your cottage, out of the way, rather than take it to the pub where we'll all have to keep looking at it and thinking about him.'

Sarah agreed, thinking how lucky Lucy was to have such a caring but level-headed friend.

Rosie slipped into the driving seat, complained how much it smelt from being shut up in the sun, opened the window and turned the key. Nothing happened so Sarah, who'd had a number of recalcitrant cars, opened the bonnet and wiggled the battery terminals.

'Try again,' she suggested, and this time the engine caught and puttered into life.

'I'll see you later,' Rosie called, then she slipped the car into gear and roared away.

By the sound of things, Lucy would be up for a new muffler before too long.

CHAPTER NINE

AS PREDICTED, the rodeo brought in its share of injuries, mostly sprains that needed ice and bandaging. One enterprising novice in the buck-jumping had shoved his feet so far into the stirrups to help him stay on that he'd been dragged around the ring behind the horse until the clowns caught the animal and released the trapped rider.

'Has this put a stop to your ambitions as a rough-rider?' Sarah asked him as she picked tiny pieces of dirt and gravel out of his face.

'I never did have ambitions,' he told her, 'but it looked so easy I thought I'd have a go. It's a good thing they put beginners on quiet horses. A real wild animal would have killed me.'

Lisa was back on duty, and she helped as Sarah flushed the wound, then examined it again through a magnifying glass, determined to get any foreign matter out of the graze so that it would heal with less scarring.

'Now, I'm going to put Betadine on it,' she told the lad. 'It will sting for a few minutes, then it will heal better if it's left open.'

'I guess I won't look any worse, walking around like this, than I would with a bandage around half my face,' he responded gloomily, when she handed him a mirror so he could check the damage. 'My mum will want to know what happened, then she'll probably finish off what the horse started.'

'Well, save yourself extra grief from her by putting a paper towel or clean rag over your pillow at night to protect the pillow slip from stains. Scabs will form over the scratches, and that's good because it keeps the wounds clean while they heal. It will be a bit red and tender, then itchy as it gets better, but if any bits get puffy or infected-looking, come back and see me.'

The young man thanked her and departed, and Lisa sighed.

'He'll probably be even more handsome with a bit of a scar down one side of his cheek,' she said.

'Are you looking for a handsome man?' Sarah asked, once again surprised by the frankness of youth.

'No, I've got one,' Lisa replied. 'But that doesn't stop me appreciating other fellows' looks.'

Charlie wandered in at that moment. Freed from drip lines and urine bag, he'd gone exploring. He had Sarah's old stethoscope around his neck. It dangled down his bare chest.

'Yo, Dr Charlie!' Lisa said to him, then she submitted to his probing, delighting the child by playing along with him.

'Do you want to get rid of him yet?' Ewan Winter appeared, looking anxious and harassed. Sarah guessed keeping someone at the hospital with Charlie wasn't easy.

'I'd rather keep him here for another day or two. It's important the wounds stay clean.'

Ewan thought about it for a moment.

'You're right, but he's missing all the fun. Could I collect him in the morning to take him to the street parade? I could carry him on my shoulders so no one jostles him. Then I'll bring him back and, if he's OK, Carey could take him home Tuesday, after the other kids have gone to school.'

'That sounds good to me,' Sarah agreed. 'We'll put a dry dressing on his back tomorrow. He's certainly healthy enough, but tell Carey, once you get him home, to bring him up each day so we can check his back, and to call me if he shows any signs of infection, runs a temp—she'd know.'

'We'd all know with Charlie,' Ewan said grimly, but when he softened the words by smiling at his small son Sarah again felt a crunching sense of need inside her.

'Phone for you, Sarah.' One of the aides poked her head into Outpatients, saving Sarah from analysing this strange new reaction she was experiencing whenever she was with the little boy. 'I've put it through to your office.'

It had to be something disastrous for sure, or the girl would have switched it to Outpatients.

She hurried through to the small room designated the doctor's office at Windrush Hospital, and found not trouble but Tony on the phone.

'The grapevine's still in working order. Someone's designated this a private call,' she told him.

'I wish it was,' he said, and she heard tiredness in his voice.

'Trouble?'

'Major!' he affirmed. 'I'm assuming Stewart had a word in the Minister's ear. Ned then got on to my police boss and told him I was out of line in pursuing inquiries into James's death.'

Sarah held her breath. It was happening again. For all his words of comfort and commitment, he was going to be whisked out of her life—as suddenly as he'd reappeared in it.

Little boys with steel grey eyes would for ever be a dream.

'So?' she said, her voice hard as she came to grips with it.

'So, I could be delayed longer than I'd hoped to be, but I'll be back, Sarah. One way or another. And, in the meantime, keep Lucy safe.'

'Keep Lucy safe?' She heard her voice rise in panic at the implication behind the words. 'Why should she not be safe?'

'If we're right about an intruder being in James's room,

and if we take that as suspicious, then once that person
finds out Lucy was in the bed she could be seen as a risk
to him or her.'

It was calm, logical, police talk, but to Sarah it combined
the wail of warning sirens with the clang of emergency
bells.

'How would he or she find out? If whoever it was didn't
see Lucy in there at the time, and we have to assume she
wasn't seen, why would the intruder suddenly assume she's
a danger?'

The silence that greeted her questions was more unset-
tling than words, although the words, when they came,
brought their own dark shadows.

'I had to tell my boss why we thought it was more than
an accident or suicide. That assumption hinges almost entirely on Lucy hearing someone in the room and our suspicions about the tampering with the label on the pill bottle.'

'But the drug tests could back us up,' Sarah reminded
him.

'Finding drugs in James's body will give more weight to
the suicide angle than to the murder theory, Sarah,' Tony
said, his voice flat and emotionless. 'Especially if we find
that the chemist made up the prescription for James, not
someone else.'

'You've changed sides,' Sarah muttered at him.

'I'm pointing out the facts,' he said, his voice as cool as
winter rain.

'But you've put Lucy in danger by mentioning her involvement! If you want to go for the suicide theory why
mention her?'

Fear for her daughter made it hard to hide her anger and
agitation.

'I mentioned it because it was the only way I could justify my continued involvement.' Even after eleven years

she could hear the stiffness in his voice and knew he was as angry as she was.

At her?

Most probably!

'Well, bully for you!' she snapped into the receiver, and dropped it onto the cradle.

Which was stupid, because she still wasn't certain how Tony telling his boss about Lucy's presence in the room...

Light dawned. If the pressure had begun at Craigmoor, the answers would go back along the same route—Tony's boss to the Minister to Stewart.

But if Lucy had seen or heard anything surely the person would assume she'd have mentioned it already—passed on whatever information she had. And, having done that, she'd no longer be a risk.

Sarah explained all this to herself as she made her way back through the hospital, but the bands of tension constricting her chest belied her own assurances and, after telling Lisa to call her on the mobile if she was needed, she walked downtown, making for the hotel, needing to see her daughter with her own eyes before she could accept she was all right.

The group were still in the corner of the beer garden, and a stack of dirty plates in the centre of the table suggested they'd eaten since Sarah had last seen them.

Lucy saw her first, and smiled.

'Checking on your chick, Mother Hen?' she teased, her voice gentle, filled with both love and understanding.

'Doing just that, my chick!' Sarah told her, and ruffled her hand through the blonde hair. 'You doing OK?'

Lucy nodded.

'We're going up to have a rest soon. Mr Todd only had one available room. In fact, it's his daughter's room but she's not here. He found a couple of old mattresses and says we can throw them down on the floor and all bunk in together. He's been really kind.'

'Most people are kind,' Sarah reminded her, hiding her relief that, even as she slept, Lucy would be surrounded by her friends. 'You're all staying on for a few days?'

She glanced around the group as she asked the question and saw the affirmative gestures.

'At least until the funeral,' Nod explained. 'Rosie told you about wanting to do the play?'

'I think it's a good idea but I'd do it after the service—outside the church.' Sarah hesitated. From a courtesy point of view they should ask permission, if not of the family then at least of the vicar, but Stewart McMurray was such a power in the area that few would agree to anything that might upset him.

Yet these young people wanted to pay their tribute to James! To have his play read aloud would have been the ultimate accolade for him.

'I'd keep quiet about it, too. When the service finishes, people usually hang about outside the church, talking to the family. Do it then.'

'Without saying anything first—is that what you mean, Mum? You think they'd stop us if we mentioned it?' Lucy honed in on the problem, then glanced at her friends. 'I guess they could at that.'

The conversation took a turn towards legalities, but Sarah felt her concern had been noted, the unspoken warning heeded, and, after a quick kiss for Lucy, she excused herself and walked away.

Then she realised she hadn't passed on Tony's caution, although while Lucy stayed within the group of friends she should be safe.

'Do you want a real drink while you're here?' Toddy called to her from the bar.

She walked into the cool, shadowed room and shook her head.

'Better not. Although the rodeo should be over by now, all the cowboys will either be celebrating their wins or drowning their sorrows over their losses. If the night ends without a fight and someone coming in to be stitched up or have their knuckles realigned I'll be pleased, but very surprised.'

'Guess you're right. I mean, considering the number of visitors in town, there's been remarkably little trouble—apart from James.'

Apart from James!

Sarah tucked the thought of him away again. Later, she silently promised him.

'With Ken out of action and only young Ryan here, perhaps it's just as well,' she said to Toddy.

'You haven't heard? Karunga sent out not one but two blokes. Both youngsters, but at least Ryan's got some company, and back-up, if trouble does break out.'

Things were looking up in the bush, Sarah decided as she walked home after thanking Toddy for his kindness to her daughter and her friends. When Tony was pulled out after Anna McMurray's death, the town had been without a policeman for two months. Of course, the local member hadn't held the police portfolio in those days.

She passed James's car, tucked in behind the sheltering screen of trees around the cottage, and made a mental note to phone a mechanic. If Lucy was going to be driving it, she wanted it in good mechanical condition.

Keep Lucy safe!

The house echoed with emptiness and she regretted her hasty termination of Tony's call.

Or the doubts and anger that had prompted it?

Had she been foolish to think that everything could be the same as it had been before Anna's death?

And after so long a time apart?

Unable to bear her own company, she turned and went back to the hospital. She'd have a talk to Mrs Rose about the alternatives open to her for future treatment. Find out what she wanted in the way of referrals.

Her patient was sitting up in bed, crocheting small squares.

'They're going to make someone a nice bright quilt,' Sarah remarked, and the older woman beamed at her.

'I can't sit around and do nothing,' she said. 'I'd be more help at my nephew's place if you sent me home. I could mind the kids.'

'You're here to rest,' Sarah reminded her. She nodded towards the photos on the locker. 'Are those your nephew's children?'

Mrs Rose reached over and selected one framed snapshot.

'This one's of his kids,' she said proudly, pointing to each smiling face and naming it. 'And this one…' She lifted another. 'These are my niece's children.'

Sarah dutifully admired them.

'Did you have no children of your own?' she asked, glancing at the other photos which all seemed older.

'Just one—my Petey. He never married. I live with him now.'

This time her nimble fingers plucked two photos off the locker.

'This is Petey!'

A tubby young man, who'd grown into an even larger older man in the second photo, beamed at her.

'He looks very nice,' Sarah said. 'Does he take care of you, or you of him?'

'Oh, Petey can look after himself,' Mrs Rose told her. 'I worked in service—out at Craigmoor, in fact—once he left school, so he learned young.'

'Out at Craigmoor?' Sarah echoed.

Mrs Rose reached for another photo and pressed it up against her breast, before passing it to Sarah.

'I looked after young James from when he was a baby. Or helped Mrs McMurray look after him. So sad, him dying that way. Like the family was cursed.'

She passed the photo in her hand to Sarah, who looked at a very young but still recognisable James.

'He was like my own,' the older woman said sadly, 'but after Alana came to stay there Mr McMurray, well, he was always saying the boy had too many women fussing over him. In the end he decided it was best I should go.'

'That must have been hard,' Sarah said, her mind racing with conjecture.

'You're telling me!' Mrs Rose, replied. 'When I'd been there that long.'

Two hours later, Sarah knew the history of Craigmoor and the life stories of both Anna and Alana, cousins who'd been brought up in very different circumstances. When Anna's parents had been killed, old James McMurray, Stewart's father and a second cousin of her mother's, had taken the child in, so Anna had grown up at Craigmoor.

Alana's father, by contrast, had been a contract bore-and-well-sinker, and the family had lived an itinerant lifestyle, travelling the outback to wherever he could get work.

'Not that you'd guess she'd grown up rough when you meet Alana,' Mrs Rose assured Sarah. 'She was that lady-like, even when she was little and came for holidays. And never jealous of her cousin. Real caring of her, all the time. Even when Mrs McMurray got so sickly.'

'What kind of sickly?' Sarah asked, and for the first time in the recital her patient hesitated.

'I don't rightly know,' she said, in a voice that had suggested she was willing to guess. 'But nowadays with all you see on these women making themselves sick to stay thin, well, I'd say that's what she had. The bully thing they talk about that Princess Di was supposed to have.'

'Bulimia?'

'That's the one. She'd eat and then she'd be sick. And, of course, Mr McMurray, he was always so strong and so fit he didn't like people being sick around him, so Alana took care of her and helped her hide how she was feeling

from him. That was at the end when she got sick—just
before I went away. Not long after you came to town, I
reckon it must have been, because I remember your little
girl coming out to play with James a couple of times.'

Sarah had a vivid image of the two children at play, Lucy
so blonde and lively, James so dark and almost sedate, even
at nine.

'They were good together,' she said softly, and Mrs
Rose, sensing her unhappiness, reached out and touched her
hand.

They sat in silence, lost in their own memories for a few
minutes, then Sarah excused herself and left. It was only
when she reached the cottage that she remembered she'd
had a purpose in going to the hospital.

Discussing Mrs Rose's future care could wait. Right now
she had to think.

She fixed herself some toast and coffee and sat down to
consider what, if anything, she'd learned.

A change in a woman after the birth of a child could
often be put down to postnatal depression, but even twenty-
one years ago that was recognised. And it hadn't happened
right after James was born. He was nine when Sarah and
Lucy had arrived in town.

No, she had to rule out postnatal depression.

Anna had been having bouts of sickness throughout the
year Sarah had been in town. And hadn't sought medical
help unless, like Alana, she regularly drove to Karunga to
see a private doctor.

Of course, if it had been bulimia, if she'd been deliberately making herself sick, it's unlikely she'd have sought
medical help. Or mentioned it to anyone.

Or if, as Tony had always said, she'd claimed she was
being poisoned, then, knowing the way gossip spread
around the town, wouldn't she have avoided doctors altogether?

Why?

In case he—or she, in this case—broke confidentiality and mentioned her visit Stewart, who, after all, had been a person of influence in the area even then?

Somehow bulimia seemed more believable than poisoning.

Sarah closed her eyes and pictured the Anna she had known. Slim, but not unnaturally so.

Had Alana been slimmer? Was there some kind of rivalry on Anna's part—a need to be thinner than her cousin?

Sarah shook her head in frustration. She'd met Alana back then, but most of her contact with the family had been with James, and through him with Anna, who would drop him off to play with Lucy or collect him when he'd visited after school.

When Lucy had been invited to Craigmoor, again it had been Anna who had welcomed and said goodbye to them, Anna who'd become a friend in the way parents of a child's playmates did.

Would the friendship have developed if Sarah's love affair with Tony hadn't enclosed her in such a bright bubble of happiness, insulating her from other people's distress?

She sighed, tipped out her cold coffee and had a glass of milk instead. As she sipped it she pondered gloomily on her own distress. More than anything, she wanted to talk to Tony—to apologise for hanging up, to share what she'd learned.

To hear his voice!

Ridiculous to think she'd fallen right back into love again with a man, and didn't even know where he lived.

She could phone Lucy at the hotel, ask for Tony's home number…

The phone rang before she could decide if that was a good or bad idea.

'I love you, you stupid woman, and nothing's going to stop us getting back together again!' the man she'd been thinking about yelled in her ear. 'And I know this is going through the hospital switchboard, but I don't even know your mobile number.'

'I was thinking the same thing—only about where you lived,' Sarah mumbled through the tears that clogged her throat.

'In Manly, a minute's walk to the beach—that do you for a city address?'

She sniffed, but it wasn't enough and she had to fish in her pocket for a handkerchief.

'Are you still there? Have we been cut off?'

'No,' she managed, in a watery voice. 'I'm crying.'

'Oh, Sarah, darling, don't cry. It rips me apart to think you're on your own up there. Don't ever cry without me around to comfort you. I'll be back just as soon as I can wangle it, but in the meantime smile for me, my darling.'

She smiled, although through a fresh flood of tears.

'I'll be all right,' she promised. 'Maybe I just needed a good cry. For James and for the past—for everything that's happened.'

She heard him chuckle.

'Well, if it's what you want, then cry away. I'll call you in the morning, OK?'

They said goodbye and rang off, but the phrase he'd used lingered in her head.

'Smile for me, my darling!'

James would have liked the words. Worked them into a play.

She glanced around the room, regretting she hadn't collected a copy of his latest play from Rosie before she'd left the hotel.

Tomorrow!

The next day arrived with brilliant sunshine, warmed by the approach of summer. Bessie had survived to take her place on the float and was already in her Sunday best, holding court for the few reporters who'd actually heard of the Windrush Sidings anniversary.

Charlie, resplendent in a fresh white shirt over his dry dressing and stethoscope slung around his neck, was waiting impatiently on the verandah for his father, while most of the staff were running around in costumes Sarah took to be those of water sprites.

'One word from you and our friendship will be finished,' Emmie warned, appearing from nowhere in a floaty chiffon creation that added about twenty pounds to her already full figure.

'I think it's very fetching,' Sarah assured her, but she couldn't hide her smile.

'All right for some,' Emmie countered, 'but the hospital couldn't be the only business in town not entering a float, now, could it?'

'Definitely not,' Sarah agreed. 'What time do you set off?'

'We're supposed to be assembling at nine o'clock for a ten o'clock kick-off to the parade but, knowing Windrush, if we get going by ten-thirty we'll be doing well.'

Sarah glanced at her watch, saw it was already nine-thirty. As the swan was still in the hospital grounds, she had to agree.

'Off you go and organise them,' she suggested. 'Someone obviously needs to be in charge.'

Emmie left, then hurried back.

'I forgot what I came in to tell you. Stewart McMurray phoned to say Alana's not feeling well. He was going to drive her into town to see you, but the motion of the car made her feel worse. He realises you're holding the fort here this morning while we're all parading but wondered if you'd have time to pop out to see her this afternoon.'

Sarah felt a momentary regret that she *was* holding the fort at the hospital. She'd have liked to have spoken to Alana on her own.

Had Stewart deliberately suggested the afternoon so he'd be there?

The idea stirred uneasily in her mind and she remembered Tony's words about Stewart's power complex.

Playing God.

'Are you OK?'

Had she shivered, that Emmie had asked the question?

She pulled herself together, smiled at her friend, assured Emmie she was well and, yes, she'd visit Alana, then sent her on her way.

Fixing her mind firmly on work, Sarah walked through to where Grant Russell provided one of two excuses for keeping the hospital open.

'Your slings and weights are all attached to the frame on your bed,' she explained to him. 'Would you like me to wheel you out on to the verandah so you can see the swan depart? I think the entire parade will pass this way eventually, although with the park in front you won't have much of a view.'

'At least I'd be outside,' Grant told her. 'And get some idea of what's going on.'

Sarah adjusted the bed's legs from stationary to wheeled position, then, moving very slowly and carefully, pushed him out of the ward into the wide corridor that ran down the centre of the hospital.

'Hey, that's my job! I was going to find you and suggest we set the lad up out the front.' Graham Logan appeared, a pair of binoculars slung around his neck. 'Brought these along so he could get a better look-see.'

Sarah thanked him and let him take over the steering of the bed. After all, he had far more experience in moving patients than she would ever have.

'Can I get you something?' she asked, when the bed was set in place. 'A drink? Snack? We might as well enjoy ourselves.'

'A cup of coffee would be nice, and some of Cook's

shortbread,' Grant said, and Sarah smiled as she wondered if all patients were offered Cook's shortbread or only the young, good-looking ones.

'I'll see to that,' Graham offered. 'Something for you, Doc?'

Sarah shook her head.

'I've not long had breakfast,' she explained.

But the mention of food made her think of Anna. Had something disturbed her to the extent that she'd stopped eating? Something to do with her husband? With his treatment of her perhaps?

No, the not eating part was wrong. Mrs Rose had said she'd eaten, then been sick after it. Had she gorged?

As soon as she finished with Grant she'd go and ask her patient.

With so many questions racing through her head, she cranked the head end of the bed up enough for Grant to see, without affecting the balance of the pulleys on his pelvis.

Concentrate on work—think about the other things later.

'And as you're out and about today, we might X-ray you later. After the parade, of course. See how the bones are knitting together. You might be nearly ready to get out of that harness.'

He agreed so wholeheartedly that she realised the inactivity had been getting him down, although he was one patient who never complained. When Graham returned with coffee and biscuits for himself and Grant, Sarah left them on the verandah and walked back to find her second patient had absconded.

'She said she was feeling well enough to go,' the aide on duty told her. 'Actually, I think she didn't want to miss the parade. Her nephew came and got her at about seven so it must have been organised.'

'Serves me right for not doing an early round,' Sarah grumbled, although she knew Mrs Rose *had* been well enough to leave. She could phone her at her nephew's to make arrangements for follow-up tests and appointments.

With no excuse to avoid it, she headed for her temporary office. No matter what she had on her mind there was always paperwork to be done, more than enough to keep her occupied until the noise of the band signalled that the parade was swinging past the hospital.

It was a quiet, uneventful morning as far as work was concerned, although the parade, as it passed, made up in noise for what it lacked in presentation. There were fourteen assorted floats in all, with the school band, the small group of marching girls and the town's brass band all providing slightly different versions of the same Australian songs.

Grant, watching through Graham's binoculars, provided a running commentary and demonstrated Bessie's regal wave.

'You must know everyone in town, the way you can pick people out,' Sarah said, when he'd listed the people on the produce store's float.

'It's from watching the cattle. When they've all got red coats and white faces, you learn to tell them by the way they move. People are just the same. You take the boss's wife, Mrs McMurray. She can ride as good as any of the men, even throw a young steer, and I've seen her cut a calf from its mother like a pro, but when she walks, even in jeans or moleskins, it's not like men walk.'

'What about Mrs Armitage? Bet you can tell her by her walk,' Graham said.

Sarah chuckled at the suggestion. Mrs Armitage was head of the hospital's women's group, which raised money and organised visitors for those folk isolated from their families.

Mrs Armitage bore down on people like an old-fashioned two-master under full sail.

Grant mentioned someone else in town with a distinctive walk, and the conversation drifted on.

By early afternoon, Bessie had come back, none the worse for her adventure, and Charlie had been returned, unscathed, to their care. Sarah was able to slip away—out to Craigmoor—although her stomach protested with uneasiness severe enough to make her wonder if there was a bug going around.

Alana was in the living room when Sarah arrived. She called to come straight in as Sarah crossed the verandah, and rose to greet her, pale and fragile-looking, waving Sarah to a chair before subsiding back onto a chaise longue.

'I'm sorry to bring you all the way out here,' Alana murmured. 'Stewart insisted I see a doctor, and now he's not here himself to talk to you.'

'Did he want to talk to me?' Sarah asked bluntly. Being in the room where she'd last spoken to James was making her feel uneasy.

Alana gave a harsh laugh.

'Well, I wanted *you* to talk to him—to assure him there's nothing wrong with me. Heavens, it's been such a traumatic few days, is it little wonder I'm feeling a bit under the weather?'

She wiped away a tear—real enough, as far as Sarah could see.

Then, ashamed of her own cynicism, she forgot she'd actually wanted to see Alana alone, and said gently, '*Is* that all it is? Have you only been feeling unwell for the last few days or has James's death simply made things worse?'

Alana sat bolt upright.

'No, no! I've been fine. I promise you, if there was something else I'd tell you. But because of the festivities, and having the official guest staying here, we've had to keep going. The ball, church service—one thing after another. I tell you, Sarah, it was more than I could do to face that damn parade today with a cheerful smile on my face. I just made out I was a bit worse than I was and Stewart went into fuss mode.'

There was a brittleness, the high pitch of near-hysteria in her voice, the tightness of strain barely under control. Sarah's uneasiness increased, and again she wondered just how far Stewart took his power complex.

'Well, I certainly can't blame you for dodging the parade. I opted out myself, but according to the message from Stewart you were physically ill this morning. I'd better at least examine you.'

She stood up and opened her bag. Examining Alana would give her more time to talk to the woman. As she slid an inflatable cuff up Alana's arm she realised she had no idea what to say—or ask.

Do you think Stewart killed his first wife? That was hardly the best conversation-starter.

'Could you be pregnant?' she settled on, deciding medical talk was easier than the investigative kind. After all, and unlikely though it seemed, having a child of her own could provide Alana with a motive for James's death. Inheritance!

'No,' Alana said flatly, slightly calmer now. 'I always knew James would be the only child I'd ever rear. I had endometriosis when I was younger, badly enough to require surgery for adhesions and then a full hysterectomy. It was after the operation that Anna invited me out here to recuperate.'

Another tear was wiped away, but Sarah, after noting down a normal temperature and BP and, if anything, a slower than normal pulse, was left feeling as if she'd missed something.

She checked the glands around Alana's neck, asked about pain or tenderness, and finally, convinced the symptoms had been, as the patient confessed, produced to get out of more socialising, she prepared to depart.

'But Stewart wanted to see you,' Alana protested. 'Stay for a cup of tea. He shouldn't be too long.'

Sarah did a mental scan of how she felt about Stewart and decided, given the suspicions she was harbouring, it would be best if they missed each other. She made an excuse of being needed at the hospital to refuse the offer.

'But he wanted to discuss funeral arrangements. I phoned Lucy for him this morning. She wasn't at the cottage. Someone said she was staying at the hotel.'

Sarah's heart began to thud. Stewart knew where Lucy was!

Lucy's safe while her friends are with her, she reminded herself, but to Alana she said, 'I really must go.'

'But the funeral!' Alana protested, and again Sarah sensed a tension in the woman. saw agitation in the nervous wringing of her hands.

Did Alana fear Stewart's wrath if she didn't keep Sarah here?

But did he want her here, or just out of town?

The thudding accelerated.

'I'm sure Stewart will do what he thinks best,' Sarah said, snapping her bag shut.

'He wants the funeral to take place on Tuesday—tomorrow—because a lot of his friends will still be in town, but he's concerned it might look rushed to the authorities,' Alana continued, following Sarah out towards the verandah, blathering on about funerals while anxiety clawed at Sarah's guts.

'Then tell him to leave it until Wednesday,' she all but snapped. 'It's probably better that way. Rather than going straight from the frivolity of the celebrations to such a stark reminder of James's death.'

There was a pause that went on too long.

'I'll tell him, though I don't know that it will help,' Alana said. 'He's devastated and, of course, if you find it was suicide, that will make things so much worse for

Stewart because he'll blame himself for putting pressure on James about coming home and learning to run Craigmoor.'

She sounded genuinely distressed but whether for Stewart or for James—or for herself—Sarah couldn't tell.

'Alana, the majority of children defy their parents' wishes at some stage of their lives, but very few commit suicide over it.'

'So, you think it *was* an accident?' Alana asked, and Sarah shrugged her shoulders.

'Only the tests will tell,' she said, hoping the words were bland enough to hide any indication of a third possibility.

'Yes.'

There was a finality in the word, and Sarah took her leave. Back at the car, she phoned the hotel. Toddy assured her the young ones were all in their room, practising some play, but, yes, he'd check on them and, no, he hadn't seen Stewart since the parade. She should have been relieved, but the anxiety that had escalated in that long, elegant room accompanied her home.

She parked beside the cottage and crossed to where James's car was standing in the shade of an old mulberry tree. Emmie's cousin was a mechanic. She'd phone him at home and ask if he'd have time to look at the car tomorrow. If it needed a part, he could get it in by Wednesday, then Lucy and her friends could drive home in convoy on Thursday, or whenever they were ready to leave.

It definitely needed a new muffler and possibly a new starter motor. She'd start it up and see.

Feeling pleased that she'd found something practical to focus on, she opened the driver's side door. The smell assailed her, not putrid—yet—but definitely unpleasant. A brief reconnaissance behind the seats revealed the remains of several fast food meals the pair must have consumed—or partly consumed—on their journey.

Holding her breath, Sarah gathered all the containers into a plastic bag and took them across to the rubbish bin. She walked back and opened the other door, but the smell lingered in the air with an unpleasant insistence so she was reluctant to get in and join it.

She checked the brake was on, pushed the gear lever into neutral, then, standing outside the driver's side so her head was above the level of the car—and out of direct line of smell—she turned the key to start the engine.

CHAPTER TEN

ANXIOUS faces swam into Sarah's vision, blurry and indistinct, mouths opening and closing, lips moving, but no sound coming out. She closed her eyes to escape the disorientation of those faces.

Now a noisy altercation was disturbing her sleep.

'Go away, it's too early.'

She thought the words, even tried to say them, but they didn't come out, although something must have happened because Lucy was there, her arms around her, tears wetting her cheeks.

Of course Lucy was crying. James was dead.

She put her arms around Lucy, and realised how awkward it was to do this lying down. She tried to sit up, and groaned as pain hit her.

Pain. That forced her mind into action. She opened her eyes again and, beyond Lucy's head, which was still pressed hard into her shoulder, she saw an unfamiliar ceiling.

She put her hands on Lucy's shoulders and eased her up, wiping at the tear-streaked cheeks. By now her other senses had revived, telling her she was in hospital. She remembered the car, the smell and a tidal wave of air hitting her with such force it must have knocked her out.

'I'm all right,' she told her distraught daughter, although she knew she wasn't because she could hardly hear her own voice and, now she was properly awake, she was aware that her entire body ached, not just her back.

'Saying it isn't enough. You'll have to prove it,' a gruff voice said, the sound echoing hollowly in Sarah's head as if the speaker were talking down a vacuum cleaner hose.

Sarah turned her head enough to see Emmie standing behind Lucy's kneeling figure. She recognised the militant expression on her friend's face.

'Were you two arguing? Is that the noise that woke me?'

It seemed so unlikely she had trouble grasping the concept.

'Emmie says you should be sent to town. Says she's not qualified to examine you properly and you need a doctor. I said you'd want to stay here. I—we—my friends and I can guard you here, Mum, make sure someone's with you all the time. We'll take care of you until Tony gets here.'

Tony was coming. The news brought such relief that Sarah let her eyes close again.

Lucy gave more justifications, and Emmie made more points, but the knowledge that Tony was on his way was enough for Sarah. To satisfy Emmie's concern, she wiggled her toes, moved her feet and legs. Groaningly, she shifted her body, but felt more aches than the sharp pains that might indicate a bone was out of place.

Bones. She didn't have to move to check her bones. Not with X-ray facilities in the hospital.

She pried her eyes open again and this time focussed them on Emmie.

'Did you X-ray me? Find anything broken?'

'Yes and no,' Emmie said reluctantly. 'But I'm not the best X-ray technician in Australia, although Mary Thomas is pretty good at reading film and she came in and said you looked all right.'

Sarah could hear Emmie's reluctance to take responsibility and knew it was because of the added concern of their friendship.

'Well, from the gross discomfort I'm feeling in another part of my anatomy, I'd say you've put in a catheter. Have you checked the bag? Any blood in my urine?'

Emmie shook her head, but refused to be placated.

'But you could have internal damage. What about a rup-
tured spleen or liver damage? You were thrown ten feet.'

'I think I'd know,' Sarah told her. 'And, even if I didn't,
we'd soon find out. Show me my chart.'

She hid a smile to see they'd been doing fifteen-minute
obs. Poor Emmie *had* been worried, although pulse and BP
were both stable.

'I look OK to me,' she said, trying to hide the pain even
breathing caused, then compromised. 'The ambulance
could have me in Karunga in little over an hour, Emmie,
if I deteriorated suddenly. But, believe me, I really would
prefer to stay here.'

'Well, you're not to think of doing any work and I'll
forbid the nurses to mention patients to you.'

Sarah nodded to show acceptance, suddenly so tired she
could barely keep her eyes open.

Then something else Emmie had said echoed in her
mind.

'Why was I thrown ten feet?' she asked.

Sarah turned towards Emmie, whose face was set in a
grim frown.

'The car blew up. I don't know why you were standing
there when it happened, but suddenly it blew up. That stupid Ryan Bourke doesn't know a thing. And nor do those
two fellows Karunga sent. I told them to put a bit of that
tape you see on TV around the whole cottage yard and just
guard it as it is until some experts arrive.'

Emmie's explanation was, no doubt, relevant, but heard
through the vacuum hose not particularly understandable.
Especially not when the first two sentences had caused
more chaos in her head.

The car blew up. That was a beauty, as sentences went.

And though Emmie didn't know why, Sarah did. She'd
started the engine.

She reached out for Lucy's hand and gripped it so tightly
her daughter winced.

'I'm staying here in Windrush,' she said to Emmie, just in case she was still in doubt. 'And Lucy's staying with me. And her friends. Phone the hotel and ask them all to come up. They can talk, keep me amused. I want them all here.'

'It's eight o'clock at night,' Emmie protested. 'You need sleep, not entertainment.'

'All of them at once, Mum?' Lucy protested. 'It will be too much for you.'

'I want them all,' Sarah insisted, and heard the quavery note of panic in her voice. She breathed deeply to settle her nerves and said to Emmie. 'I'll still sleep, but I want to know they're around—that Lucy's got someone with her when I sleep.'

Emmie would think that was OK because Lucy was still grieving.

Wouldn't she?

No time to argue. Keep talking!

'The hospital kitchen can provide their meals,' Sarah added, to reinforce her decision, 'and bill me later for the cost.'

Lucy opened her mouth to argue again, and Sarah resorted to blackmail. This time she let the tears she'd been holding back flow freely. She turned to the precious daughter she'd so nearly lost and said, 'I want you with me all the time. Please, darling.'

This time it was Lucy's turn to be comforter. She put her arms around Sarah's shoulders, smoothed her hair and whispered soothing words.

'I won't leave you, Mum,' she said. 'I promise. I'll be right here. You try to rest.'

Rest? When someone's trying to kill my daughter? How can I rest?

She could hear hysteria rising in her head. Knew she couldn't handle it, handle any of this. Not on her own.

'When's Tony coming?' she asked, or thought she asked, but couldn't have because no one answered.

She opened her eyes again, and saw what looked like fear in Lucy's pale, shocked face.

'Soon, Mum. He'll be here soon,' she said.
Although Sarah wondered if her daughter was simply pacifying her, she knew, for Lucy's sake—to ease *her* tension—she had to pretend to be placated by it.

'OK,' she said, and closed her eyes again. But there was no way she was going to sleep, because if she did she might let go of Lucy's hand and she'd slip away—into some new and terrible danger.

They must have drugged her, because staying awake proved near impossible, so 'awake' became a relative state. She was aware that Lucy's friends had come because she heard their voices as they read through James's play. Not that she could make much sense of it in her all but comatose state. It was about a very kind woman, as far as she could gather. One of the boys was reading the part they'd designated Sarah's.

If she was better.

She would play the very kind woman—or was Lucy playing that part? Perhaps she'd be the one who died. It all seemed very strange but in her mind she connected it to Anna and Alana, although in the play it seemed it was the child who killed the woman.

She drifted again, and, realising she must have slept, woke to clasp the hand in hers even more tightly. Except it wasn't Lucy's hand—far too large, far too firm.

The room was dark, filled with shadows and someone who wasn't Lucy. Sarah struggled to sit up, snatching at her hand, searching the shadows.

'Where is she? Where's Lucy? I told her she had to stay. Had to be here, right beside me. With her friends. Where's she gone?'

The mattress sagged as a heavy body settled on its edge, and warm, familiar hands gripped her shoulders.

'It's OK, my darling,' Tony's voice assured her. 'You kept her safe, kept her by you until I got here. She's back at the cottage with her friends. It was easier to guard them there than at the hotel where so many people go in and out. I've a couple of police on duty outside the cottage. They'll keep watch throughout the night.'

The relief was so great she almost cried again.

'You knew? Guessed? Emmie said the car just blew up—they all assumed I was unlucky, but I started it, Tony. I started the engine. It could have been Lucy!'

'I know, my darling. I know.' His voice was harsh and thick as if he, too, was close to tears, and he added, 'Or you.' His arms tightened around her shoulders and she knew he'd felt the fear for her that she'd felt for her daughter.

'They'd left old food scraps in it. It stank to high heaven. I could no more have sat in it than flown to the moon, but I thought I'd check if the engine would start. I wanted everything fixed if Lucy was to be driving it.'

She pressed her body against his as the horror of what had so nearly happened overwhelmed her. Tony's chest was hard and solid, his arm around her both tender and comforting.

Yet she had to know.

'It *was* deliberate?'

'I think so,' he replied. 'I flew back up with some fellows from the bomb squad and a guy who'll act as temporary replacement for Ken while he's hospitalised. I've also brought all the results of the tests the lab had run. There are more to come, of course, things that take longer, but preliminary testing shows James had taken or been given a large amount of butobarbitone.'

Confirmation. But of what?

'And?' she prompted, and he chuckled.

'You're supposed to be an invalid. Kept worry-free.'

'As if!' she muttered, but she felt an inner thrill that someone cared about her health and welfare after so many years alone.

'Wherever the label had rubbed off, it wasn't in James's toilet bag. The lads found traces of many weird things in the bag, but no trace of that type of paper. I've spoken to his friends today, and he's used that same toilet bag for years. It was a present from his father when James first went to university, and he was a sentimental young man for all their differences of opinion.'

'And the bottle itself?'

'No evidence that it was used for anything but the tablets on the label. The experts are still working on the label itself and a local detective in Armidale will be visiting the chemist as soon as they've narrowed down the various combinations of what's left of the identifying number. I spoke to the chemist, and the first few digits change monthly so one of the code-breakers at the lab is working up a bigger list of possibilities than Lucy had for him to try.'

'And in the meantime?' she asked, her body relaxing sleepily against his strength and warmth.

'The bomb chaps collect the remnants of the car engine and start looking at what caused it. Their first impression is gelignite, and as odd sticks of gelly can be found in sheds on properties in most country areas—it was always used for blasting out old tree stumps—that doesn't take us much further.'

A shadow of an idea flashed across Sarah's mind, but although she probed, trying to isolate and strengthen it, she couldn't recapture it.

'But how?'

Tony hesitated, then, perhaps realising she couldn't rest with so much unanswered, explained.

'The simplest car bomb would be a few sticks of gelly with a detonator stuck in them, taped or wired to the underside of the car, under the passenger seat or, for a really fiery conflagration, to the fuel tank.'

Sarah hid her shiver of alarm as he continued.

'Fortunately for you, whoever did it didn't think of that, and, according to the chap who took a quick look earlier, simply shoved a few sticks in the engine somewhere. A wire is then run from the detonator to the coil, and starting the engine completes the circuit.'

'Then why didn't it explode when Rosie drove it?'

She asked the question haltingly because the possibility she might have caused Rosie's death was almost too much to accept.

'It can't have been set up at that time. The actual explosive may have been put in place, somewhere inconspicuous, but the wiring almost certainly happened later.'

'Because whoever did it didn't want it exploding at Craigmoor? Alana was ill but Stewart was in town that morning.'

The shiver became a tremble as the full implication of what had happened struck her with a horrifying force. Then she thought of something else.

'Have you confirmed that the Minister passed on your information about Lucy being in the bedroom?'

Tony's arms tightened around her, and he pressed a kiss against her cheek.

'To put you and Lucy in such danger! I can't believe I did it! Pompous ass that I was. Blurting out our suspicions in an attempt to justify my own position so I could come back and sort it out officially.'

'You had to do it,' Sarah told him. 'Without that tiny element of doubt, the tests would have come back and any coroner would rule either suicide or accidental death. Death by misadventure. As good as saying we don't know any more than that he took tablets, drowned and died. That's not the way for James to go, and we'll prove it.'

Tony chuckled at her vehemence.

'For a badly shaken lady, you're pretty feisty!' Then his voice deepened as he asked, 'Are you OK? Emmie said you insisted on staying here, and I know you did that for Lucy, but should you go to town now I'm here to look after her? The force of the blast—your body took a terrible thump.'

Again the warmth of being cared for flooded through her stiff and aching muscles.

'I'll survive,' she said. 'No, I'll do more than that. I'll be well enough to go to James's funeral tomorrow and I'll read my part in the play.'

'James's funeral is today. It's after midnight,' Tony said gently. 'You've been out of it all day.'

Not quite, she wanted to tell him, but suddenly there were more important things to be said.

'I love you.'

He hugged her closer and she felt his lips move against her hair.

'You're concussed,' he teased. 'You shouldn't say too much in case you regret it later.'

'I won't regret it later and I'm going to say it often. At least once a day, and probably more often, because life's too short to not share the really good things.'

'Like love?'

She snuggled up against him.

'Like love!'

CHAPTER ELEVEN

BECAUSE Sarah was too weak to fight Lucy, Emmie and Tony when all three banded against her, and because she was in more pain than she was willing to admit, she attended James's funeral in a wheelchair.

The religious minister gave a long and sonorous speech about youth cut off in its prime, then the political one took advantage of a bit of extra publicity by speaking fulsomely about the McMurrays—more in praise of Stewart and Alana than of James.

A mournful hymn, which Lucy refused to sing because she'd phoned Stewart to tell him the kind of songs James would have liked at his funeral and had been ignored, wound up the proceedings.

As Jill and Winkle manoeuvred her wheelchair out of the church, Sarah looked around for Tony. He'd left at dawn, muttering about work he had to do, but had promised to be present for the service.

She couldn't see him, but smiled to herself when she realised she wasn't panicking about his absence, secure in the knowledge he wouldn't let her down. Today or ever.

Now she had the faith she hadn't had eleven years ago— the trust she'd denied him back then.

'OK, we're on,' Rosie whispered, as Nod stood tall on the top step of the church and spoke to the mourners, who'd reached level ground and were milling about as they waited to speak to the family. Stewart was closest, Alana towards the back of the crowd, no doubt moving people on with swift efficiency.

'Please, people,' Nod called, in a voice that carried so effortlessly that Sarah knew this wasn't his first public performance. 'You all heard that James had been honoured to be in the running for the Young Playwright of the Year, but those of you who live out here may never have had the opportunity to judge his talent for yourselves.'

He paused, aware he had everyone's attention.

'We, his friends, would like to extend to you that privilege. We have here his latest work, a draft of a short one-act play he'd been working on when he died. It's not complete, but the words are there. James's words. The play is called *Chinese Whispers*.'

Sarah saw a movement in the crowd and sensed tension building like static electricity in the air. She spotted Tony. He'd joined Alana who was working her forward through the gathering so she could join her husband. Was Tony sticking with her because he feared she, too, might be in danger? Surely not in this crowd.

Sarah opened her script, determined not to let the others down. The bits she had to read were highlighted in red—like blood—and she had to force herself to concentrate on the other voices so she wouldn't miss her cue.

"'I can't be blamed for actions taken so many years ago,'" she read aloud. "'By others, not by me.'"

Lucy took up her part, speaking in her clear young voice.

Then Nod, the child, crying because Jill was sent away, Lucy comforting him but in some way intimating it was all Sarah's fault.

Sarah felt her heart begin to hammer against her ribs as the words took on a life of their own, painting a picture too terrible to view.

She glanced desperately around. The young ones read on, oblivious to any hidden meaning. She found Tony's face, towards the front now, his hand resting lightly on Alana's elbow.

He nodded, as if to acknowledge Sarah's presence, but something in that nod confirmed the terrible knowledge seeping into her soul.

Lucy, in her part, moved closer, took Sarah's hand and said, "'Let's go and see the water together. Let's watch the tidal wave of destruction sweep across this poisoned place.'" Sarah shrank back from her daughter.

"'It's not the water but the stories,'" Nod cried, his voice a child's—a fearful child's.

"'Drink your milk,'" Lucy read, "'and go to sleep. In the morning, you'll know it was a dream.'"

"'But did I?'" Nod continued, his voice older now. "'Did I dream that death? Did I dream cries of pain so sharp they cut through drugged innocence? Dream the pain and water, the death beneath the tide?'"

His voice faded on the questions and the others grouped together to whisper stories that would pass from one person to another. Whisper, whisper, whisper, muffled inaudible words, yet the audience remained immobile, as if waiting for something to happen. Then, from a huddle, the five young people formed into a line. This was where they passed the whisper from one to the next, each changing it slightly until it was unrecognisable.

Lucy, first in line, stepped forward.

"'The story started and ended with me. In the beginning, it went like this.'" She was reading the words, her head bent over the script, so she didn't see the figure break from the crowd and dash up the steps.

Someone cried out, but Alana McMurray already had her hands around Lucy's throat, bearing her down to the ground, pounding her head against the brick paving.

'Stop her!' Sarah cried, catapulting her body out of the wheelchair and staggering towards her daughter. But Tony was ahead of her, and Nod and Winkle. Between them they pulled Alana back, releasing Lucy who was helped to a sitting position by Jill and Rosie.

Sarah knelt beside her, her shaking hands no use in checking out her daughter.

'I'm OK, Mum,' Lucy told her. 'Tony warned us something might happen. We were kind of ready for it.'

She smiled a wobbly kind of smile, and squeezed Sarah's hand.

But hand squeezes didn't do much for a rising anger.

'Tony told you this might happen?' Sarah said, unable to believe what she'd heard.

A better smile from Lucy this time. Almost cheeky.

'He read the script we left for you. I'd put Stewart into the role of the big bad wolf and I bet you had, too. Tony says he doesn't ever leap to conclusions over anything in an investigation, which is just another way of saying he wasn't going to tell us who he suspected.'

'Men!' Sarah muttered, but before she could add a few other criticisms Lucy was talking again.

'Anyway, after reading the play, he decided it might be an allegorical reconstruction of James's mother's death. The part Jill read was the woman who'd worked for the McMurrays when James was a baby, and the part Winkle read was Stewart who was hearing the stories from Rosie. Rosie's part represented all the townspeople who gossiped and spread the stories.'

Sarah, who'd reached the same conclusion herself, but much later as she'd listened to it all unfold outside the church, brushed the explanation impatiently away.

'And Tony, suspecting this, let you go ahead and do it?' she demanded.

'He thought it might flush Alana out,' Lucy told her, adding, as she touched the emerging bruises on her neck, 'And it worked.'

'She c-could have k-killed you!' Sarah stuttered, so angry with Tony that murder seemed too good a way for him to die.

'Or you, Mum, with the car. Remember that!' Lucy hugged her tightly. 'We couldn't let her get away with it.'

Sarah sighed. Lucy was right, but that didn't make her feel any less antsy towards Tony Kemp.

She was about to say so when Emmie appeared.

'Come on, the party's over,' the nursing sister said briskly. 'I'm taking you back to the hospital.' She turned to Nod and Winkle.

'If I get her back into her transport, could you two strong lads lift the chair down the steps?'

Sarah protested at this treatment, but when she stood up her knees were so weak she was glad to slump back into her 'transport'.

Once they were back on level ground, Lucy bent and kissed her.

'The others are going up to the pub to drink a toast to James. Will you be OK? I could come and sit with you.'

Sarah smiled at her daughter's concern. Much as she wanted to be with her friends for their private wake for James, duty tied her to her mother.

'Have a drink for me,' Sarah said, waving them all away. 'And don't decide it would be a good idea to visit me later in the day when you've all had a few. There's nothing worse than being the only sober one with a group of drunks who think their conversation is either hilarious or incredibly deep and meaningful.'

'Well, I like that!' Lucy said huffily, then she grinned and bent to kiss her mother. 'I shall see you in the morning,' she promised. 'No, not too early. I know you don't do mornings. Though how you can avoid them in a hospital where everything starts rattling at daybreak…'

Emmie protested that she ran a very quiet hospital, and they moved off in convoy, Winkle steering the wheelchair, Emmie giving orders and the others talking about the last act of the funeral.

'I do hope James was up there, looking down,' Nod said. 'It was such a dramatic coup. The best ending he could ever have imagined. How he'd have loved the audience participation! Talk about bringing theatre to the people!'

Sarah heard Lucy sniff, and wiped away a tear herself, but Nod was right. James would have loved it!

She was pleased to be hustled back into the hospital, so exhausted she let Emmie fuss over her.

'What's this?' she demanded, as Emmie helped her into a new and most attractive nightdress—well, more a confection of satin and lace than a nightdress.

'Lucy brought it up. Said it was a present from James, but she'd prefer you had it. She was going to stick to his cast- off T-shirts for a while yet.'

Once again, there were tears to blink away.

'I must be getting soft,' she scolded herself, and Emmie patted her shoulder.

'Or you're sicker than you'll admit,' she said. 'Now rest. Tony will be busy sorting out all that's happened and seeing everything's done right, but we both know he'll be here just as soon as he can make it.'

'So that's why I'm all decked out like a sacrificial lamb!' Sarah yelled, bolting upright in the bed then regretting it as pain stabbed in her back and her head throbbed viciously.

'I want to kill him, not seduce him!' she told Emmie.

'Well, it doesn't hurt to look nice while you're doing it,' Emmie replied. 'I mean, you only have to take a look at Alana to know what a well-dressed murderer is wearing!'

Sarah shuddered, and Emmie was immediately contrite.

'I'm sorry, I shouldn't have said that. But I'm so cross with myself that *I* believed the stories she spread, and *I* was taken in by her charm and kindness. I comforted you at the time, but I believed Anna had had an affair with Tony. It was all so damn convincing!'

Sarah relaxed back against the pillows.

'I know,' she said soberly. 'But to think that all that anger was there, simmering beneath that polished veneer she wore like armour. The envy that Anna had been brought up in the nice house, married the wealthy man, borne a son. It must have seemed unfair that Anna should have so much while Alana had so little.'

'Unfair isn't enough to kill people!' Emmie reminded her. 'Did she think of fairness when she killed James? Or blew you up, trying to kill Lucy?'

'That could have been an accident,' Sarah reminded her, and Emmie huffed and puffed as if to blow the suggestion away.

'No way! That woman grew up with explosives.'

The fragment of an idea Sarah had tried to capture when she'd spoken to Tony clicked into place as Emmie continued.

'Her father used them in his work and she always helped him. And Grant saw her in the hospital grounds while the parade was going on. Said she was wearing old work pants and a wide Akubra bush hat, but he knew her walk.'

Sarah closed her eyes, remembering Grant talking about the way Alana walked. It had crossed Sarah's mind at the time that he might have been interested in his boss's wife, but she hadn't guessed he'd mentioned her because he'd seen her there that day!

'You're tired,' Emmie said gently. 'I'll go away. Have a sleep. You look pale but still ravishing. Just don't get blood on the nightgown!'

'Ah, the beautiful but murderous sacrificial lamb.'

Tony's voice brought Sarah out of a light doze, and she glanced around, surprised to see the room shadowed by dusk. Perhaps it hadn't been such a light doze!

'You've been talking to Emmie!' she said, hiding her delight at seeing him behind a cross tone.

'I've been talking to most of the town,' he said, and she heard the weariness in his voice and saw his lack of sleep in the dark shadows beneath his eyes. Then he half smiled and her heart turned over.

'You'll be pleased to hear that most of them have assured me they never did believe the stories about myself and Anna!'

'Not much they didn't!' Sarah muttered, angry for his sake now. 'And, speaking of the townsfolk, was that real-life drama necessary? Wouldn't science have found the evidence you needed? Did you have to put Lucy at such risk?'

'Lucy chose to do it, Sarah. She's a woman and entitled to make up her own mind no matter how much you wish to protect her.'

He spoke firmly, but he took her hand and bowed his head over it, pressing it against his lips.

'Except when Lucy phoned to tell me you'd been injured,' he said huskily, 'I doubt if I've ever felt as frightened as I was when Alana dashed forward. Do you think I could have forgiven myself if anything had happened to Lucy? I was keen to see the effect of the "whispers" on the town—to see if the stories did spread—but not if it meant putting that precious girl at risk.'

'Keen because you suspected Alana might crack? Confess?'

'I've seen enough wrong-doers who are almost pleased when they're caught—as if they're relieved they can stop pretending to be something they're not—to hope it might happen. But I also thought it might trigger memories of Anna's death in someone else, bring out some new facts so we could settle that matter as well.

'As far as James's death was concerned, we were slowly gathering enough evidence to make a case against Alana without a confession. The bomb experts tell me they expect to find fingerprints on the paper wrappings they've collected. Ryan Bourke and one of the new policemen from Karunga went out to Craigmoor and searched the gardens beds near the pool. They found a cut piece of tile that could have been used to make the mark on James's temple.'

'I suppose whatever she used had to be handy—she was taking such a risk at that stage anyway.' Sarah studied his face, wondering how it would feel to be a policeman. 'Did you hold her there? Outside the church?'

'I encouraged her to stay. She was edging away when I arrived. Made some excuse about going back to the house to see to the food, so I guessed then she'd read the play.'

'But James was still working on it. When could she have read it?' Sarah demanded, surprised to find everything was finally falling into place.

'Stewart told me they were in Armidale for Wool Week and, although James wasn't there, Alana went to his flat one day to drop off a new jersey they'd bought for him. James could have had a printout of the first draft lying around the place. She's talking—raving, really. Going on and on about James accusing her of murder. If she'd read a copy, she might have seen it that way and decided she'd have to get rid of James. The prescription was dated at that time, and she had another bottle of the same tablets in her collection so it's something regularly prescribed for her use.'

Sarah nodded, as more pieces of the puzzle fitted together.

'But she must have started planning straight away, or do murder plots arrive, fully fledged, in people's minds? I mean, she must have been thinking pretty far ahead to visit a chemist in Armidale to get the right label on the bottle.'

Tony considered this for a moment.

'It was more likely to be fortuitous. She may have left her sleeping tablets at home, so had the new script filled while she was there. Then, as she's trying to work out how to either stop publication of the play—an unlikely scenario given James's sudden success—or get rid of James, it occurred to her it could be useful.'

'Get rid of James? It's so damned cold-blooded.'

'She'd killed before,' Tony reminded her. 'Everything we read tells us it gets easier. Particularly if it meant protecting her position, not to mention her freedom!'

Sarah sighed.

'Is it all over?' she asked.

He nodded.

'For a time. Alana's being flown to Sydney for psychiatric evaluation. Stewart can afford the best for her, so she'll be well looked after until she comes to trial. If she comes to trial. At the moment she certainly seems mentally unstable—now everything's come unstuck. In fact, the way she tried to tie up loose ends after killing James, showed signs of panic, of a mental deterioration that was close to desperation.'

'Loose ends like Lucy?' Sarah shuddered.

'And substituting bicarbonate of soda for the flour at the hamburger stall at the school fête. Apparently, her contribution had been the ingredients for the hamburgers. She phoned the parents' and citizens' committee president next day to tell her it was an accident. Her story was that she was so upset about James she brought the wrong container into town and realised her mistake when she heard about people being ill. My guess is that it was insurance. If you were busy with a lot of nauseated patients at the hospital, maybe you'd skimp on the autopsy. Go with what was easy.'

'Death by misadventure!' Sarah muttered, then saw the weakness in the argument. 'But I'd finished the autopsy long before the lunchtime fiasco.'

'Only because Lucy woke early, went looking for James and raised the alarm—then phoned you herself. If she'd woken later, or not gone outside... If one of the other guests had found James, perhaps at eight o'clock...'

'You're right. In fact, had Lucy not been there, who knows what might have happened in the way of delays or collusion?' Sarah let it all sink in—too many answers where once there'd been too many questions. 'And the urn being knocked over at the hamburger stall delayed things even more. The woman in charge was hospitalised so the hamburger preparation began later than expected.'

She thought of something else. Another detail.

'What about Ken?'

Tony grinned at her.

'That was our paranoia showing. The lab found no sign of anything but a blow-out. And if you think about it logically, having set up such a great scenario to cover the suicide angle if accidental death didn't work, she'd hardly want to stop the samples reaching town.'

He put his arms around Sarah and held her for a moment, and she thought about all the hours of being close they'd missed.

'And Stewart? Did he suspect her? Was that why our taking the cups from the house upset him so much?'

Tony shook his head.

'He says not, and I believe him. If you consider the kind of man he is, proud and upright—overly conscious of his standing in the community and keeping up appearances. He's also a man who's convinced his way is not just the right way but the only way to go. His arguments with James were all about James's refusal to walk the path his father had chosen for him.'

'You're saying his reaction to an investigation was predictable. He didn't want the family name sullied with talk of suicide, so decided in his own mind James's death was an accident?'

'And, having decided that, he didn't want any foolish women doctors trying to prove otherwise,' Tony teased, running his hand lightly over her hair.

Sarah was tempted to give in to the caress, to snuggle up against him and allow their mutual attraction to blank the horrors from her mind. But too many questions remained unanswered.

'Do you think he took the same tack over Anna's death? Went for the accident theory, drowned by flood waters, to avoid any hint of scandal?'

'Any more scandal,' Tony reminded her. 'The rumours broke so suddenly he was powerless to stop them. He must have seen the flood as a blessing because it diverted everyone's attention, and by the time the waters receded he was a widower and deserving of a more worthy pity, in his eyes, than a wronged husband would have been.'

Sarah nodded slowly, remembering the scenario and fitting together a few more of the missing bits of the jigsaw.

'How's Stewart now?'

Tony looked grim.

'Shattered is the only word to describe him. It's as if the earth had suddenly started spinning in a different direction. From the way he spoke, his marriage to Alana was more "suitable" and "convenient" than a great love match. He needed a wife, his child needed a mother, it was the right thing to do. He knew she was what he calls "highly strung"—'

'Yes, he told me earlier she had enough tablets to stock a chemist's shop,' Sarah mused. 'He must have accepted she needed sedatives to help her run on an even keel.'

Tony grinned at her.

'We come back to him always being right, don't we? As he'd married her it *must* have been the correct decision, so he'd turn a blind eye to her taking whatever was necessary for her to play the part of the first lady of Windrush.'

'And looking at his character again, there's no way he'd have married her in the first place if he'd had any suspicion she was implicated in Anna's death,' Sarah said slowly. 'So where would James have found the idea for his play? Why would he have been suspicious? And why speak now? And in such a way?'

Once again Tony brushed his hand across her hair, then slid his knuckles down her cheek.

'Nod filled that bit in for me,' he said, his eyes grave and full of shadows. 'Apparently Nod had a disrupted childhood, brought up in various foster homes. One of the psychology lecturers at the university talked generally about repressed memory—the pros and cons of what's seen as a new science—and happened to mention a psychiatrist in Sydney who specialised in it.

'James urged Nod to go, but he refused to believe there was anything in it. Reckoned it was a lot of rubbish and the bad stuff in your life should stay right where it was—buried as deeply as possible. In the end James offered to go with him. They'd both have a turn, see what the fellow might dig up, then make their own judgements as to whether there was any truth in it or not.'

Sarah drew in a very deep, slow breath as the enormity of what had happened suddenly struck her.

'I've always been very sceptical of it,' she muttered. 'Although, in James's case, I know he was tormented by his mother's death. I put it down to that guilt feeling you get when someone close to you dies—you wonder if you could have saved them. If a juxtaposition of circumstance—you being there, for instance—could have diverted fate.'

She shook away bad memories.

'Did he talk about it later? Tell Nod what came out of the session?'

Tony's fingers were now caressing her neck and she had to work harder on her concentration.

'He agreed with Nod's judgement that it was all hogwash, but he went back to Sydney not long after that—on business connected with his play, possibly he see the specialist again. We have the name and will check.'

'But, in the meantime, he put it all down in fictionalised form before he went,' Sarah said slowly. 'And left a copy on his desk!'

'He might have needed to do that to get it out of his system,' Tony suggested. 'We don't know that he was ever going to rock the boat by making his work public.'

'And upsetting his father even more than he already had,' Sarah agreed. 'Poor James. And poor Stewart. What will become of him?'

'I believe he might find an inner strength he never realised he had,' Tony replied. 'He's already looking inside himself, questioning some of those rigid values he's held so dear for so long. It's a hard way to learn, but I'm confident he'll face the ordeal that lies ahead with courage and come out the other end a better man.'

'But he'll still retain enough of his old values, the good bits of them, to stand by Alana while she needs him.' Sarah shuddered as she said the name. 'I know I should feel pity for Alana, but she not only took my lovely James, and hurt Lucy so badly, she also tore you and me apart for no other reason than to smear her cousin's name with dirt and mask her own crime.'

Tony bent and brushed a kiss across her lips.

'Feel sorry for me if you have to feel sorry for anyone,' he said softly.

She steeled herself against the pleasure that stole into her bones and made her stomach cramp with need.

'Sorry for you? Why?'

'Because I've had no sleep for about three days, no sex for eleven years and you're still cross with me, I can tell.'

'Yes, I am,' she said, but she kissed him anyway. Then, when the kiss had deepened to the stage where it stole her breath completely, she pushed herself away.

'No sex for eleven years? I don't believe it. There must have been someone in all that time?'

Grey eyes, already dark with passion, looked into hers.

'Was there for you?'

She shook her head.

'Not that I didn't get offers,' she told him firmly. 'I just couldn't fancy anyone enough to make the commitment.'

'Me, too,' he said softly, then he kissed her again, holding her gently so the bruises didn't hurt, although she was soon so thoroughly anaesthetised by desire she doubted whether she'd have felt them.

EPILOGUE

'JAMES and I have had a sibling meeting and decided we don't know why you're dragging us to this God-forsaken country town to get him christened,' Lucy complained.

Sarah twisted in her seat and saw Lucy bent over the baby capsule, trailing her hair temptingly towards her half-brother—the child she'd decided should be called James.

Lucy was smiling as the baby's chubby hands waved ineffectively in the air, trying to grasp the tempting strands. It was good to see Lucy smiling again, regaining her zest for life—even though that zest was tempered by a new maturity.

'We're going because it was here I began to think about love and trust, here I decided to contact Tony again—even before he was catapulted back into my life.'

Tony lifted one hand from the steering-wheel and touched her lightly on the knee.

She smiled to hide the physical reaction even so casual a touch could trigger.

'So, tell us again who'll be there,' Lucy suggested. 'James has trouble remembering all the names.' She gave a shriek as James's hands finally connected, and tugged hard. 'Don't you, brat?' she added fondly.

'We'll be staying with Andrew and Jessica Kendall. They've just completed extensions to their house so they have plenty of space. Jess is pregnant—due in a couple of weeks. My other friends, Abby and Iain McPhee, have a little girl who's going on for two. Abby's also pregnant.'

'Gross! Everyone breeding madly!' Lucy snorted.

'Except us!' Tony reminded her. 'We already have our

family—one girl and one boy. What more would anyone want?'

Lucy chuckled.

'You're only saying that because you suffered more than Mum right through her pregnancy. You were a mess from the very beginning.'

Tony threw her a severe glance.

'I was *not* a mess!' he said firmly. 'I was worried for her sake.'

'And if you mention my age, I'll hit you!' Sarah warned, smiling to herself because she knew his obvious concern—and his constant fussing, which had nearly driven her mad—had been an indication of the depth of his love.

They were approaching Riverview and she gave directions, finally indicating that Tony should stop outside the cottage.

It looked the same, the garden a riot of spring colour, the mellow stone offering a welcome, although beyond the original building she could see the roofline of the new extensions.

The front door opened, and familiar faces appeared. Jess led the way, her dark hair flying, her face dusky with late pregnancy, but her beauty not in any way diminished by her bulk. Abby followed more slowly, and Sarah guessed this pregnancy wasn't going any more smoothly than the first had. Iain was behind her, a blonde-haired mite perched on his arm. Then came Andrew, smiling with pride and delight.

Sarah was glad he'd stayed a friend.

'Who's the hunk?' Lucy whispered to her mother as they both worked to extricate James from the capsule.

Sarah twisted around to see a third man, hanging back, part but not part of this welcome. He was tall, with dark mahogany hair and a clear, fair skin that suggested he hadn't seen much sun in his life.

'That must be Iain's brother. He's out from Scotland.

Staying with them for a while,' Sarah said, and was amused
to see that Lucy had stopped helping her with James and
was hurriedly applying lip-gloss.

'I'll get the baby, you talk to your friends,' Tony suggested, leaning in to see what they were doing. He caught
Lucy's surreptitious actions and cocked his eyebrows at
Sarah, then he nodded, as if to confirm that the young
woman they both loved was finally reclaiming life.

Sarah left them to it, and turned to greet her friends,
exchanging hugs and kisses, seeing their happiness in shining eyes and glowing skin—sensing the deep contentment,
the inner peace and the inexplicable excitement that love
offered as gifts to a committed relationship.

Trust, love and marriage. It hadn't been easy, but it had
finally worked out for all of them, and the dreams of 'happy
ever after' were most definitely in place.

MILLS & BOON®

Makes any time special™

Mills & Boon publish 29 new titles every month. Select from...

Modern Romance™   Tender Romance™

Sensual Romance™

Medical Romance™   Historical Romance™

MAT2

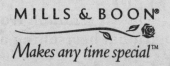

MILLS & BOON®

Makes any time special™

St. Elizabeth's
Children's Hospital

ONLY £2.99

A limited collection of 12 books. Where affairs of
the heart are entwined with the everyday dealings
of this warm and friendly children's hospital.

Book 4
Second Lover by Gill Sanderson
Published 4th August

SECH/RTL/2c

*Available at branches of WH Smith, Tesco,
Martins, RS McCall, Forbuoys, Borders, Easons,
Volume One/James Thin and most good paperback bookshops*

The latest triumph from
international bestselling author

Debbie Macomber

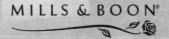

brings you

PROMISE

*Share the lives—and loves—of the
people in Promise, Texas.
A town with an interesting past
and an exciting future.*

Available from 21st July